Kings and Sages

Gavin St. pg 96
Doc Young ? pg 125

Kings and Sages

Ann,
May you always —
Be More Happy!

LSBeck

L. S. Beck

5-29-2010

iUniverse, Inc.
New York   Bloomington

Kings and Sages

Copyright © 2010 by L. S. Beck

All rights reserved. No part of this book may be used or reproduced by any means, graphic, electronic, or mechanical, including photocopying, recording, taping or by any information storage retrieval system without the written permission of the publisher except in the case of brief quotations embodied in critical articles and reviews.

iUniverse books may be ordered through booksellers or by contacting:

iUniverse
1663 Liberty Drive
Bloomington, IN 47403
www.iuniverse.com
1-800-Authors (1-800-288-4677)

Because of the dynamic nature of the Internet, any Web addresses or links contained in this book may have changed since publication and may no longer be valid. The views expressed in this work are solely those of the author and do not necessarily reflect the views of the publisher, and the publisher hereby disclaims any responsibility for them.

ISBN: 978-1-4502-1288-5 (sc)
ISBN: 978-1-4502-1289-2 (ebook)
ISBN: 978-1-4502-1290-8 (dj)

Library of Congress Control Number: 2010901613

Printed in the United States of America

iUniverse rev. date: 02/16/2010

For Gordon, who is my everything.

Happy hearts and happy faces,
Happy play in grassy places,
That was how, in ancient ages,
Children grew to kings and sages.

—From *The Children's Hour*, R. L. Stevenson

Author's note:

Many years ago, when I was a very small girl, I knew an old man. His name was Be More Happy. Actually, that's just what we called him because it was painted across the back of his old truck, and we didn't know what his real name was. He was what most people would call a hermit, only I knew he didn't mean to be like that. I knew he was hurting inside, so he just kept to himself. How did I know this? Probably, it was the look in his eyes. That is why you must always remember to look a person in the eye when you talk to them. Many people don't say what they feel. You have to read it on their faces. Anyway, this old man became a friend to all of us, me and my friends. He taught us that it wasn't *who* we were, but *what* we were that counted in life. And *that*, my friend, was a most important lesson. Funny enough, it didn't come from a book or from our lessons at school. So watch out, you may be learning by just walking down the street. Keep your eyes open. And remember, this happened a long time ago, in a faraway place. People talked differently and lived differently than they do today.

The wheels screamed, metal on metal, and slowly drew to a stop. A train is certainly no place to get a restful night's sleep. I sat up and leaned my aching head against the icy cold window, and there, between the leafless trees and through the bushes, along the river bank, I could see children playing. It was freezing cold, but I saw in their faces something I had lost. Three of the children were on their hands and knees beside the river, looking intently after something in the water. The fourth, a girl, held her face to the sky, her eyes closed and her long dark hair flying wildly with the wind. Her cheeks were red, and she clutched a worn denim jacket to her neck with hands that were white with cold. She seemed not only to savor but to cling to every minute of her freezing agony. As the train started to move again, I thought of a summer day, long gone, and of an old man called *Be More Happy*. I could smell the dust rising up around my bare feet. I could hear the voices …

Chapter 1

"Last one to hit has to eat a worm!" Danny dared them all. Just then, I looked up to see a trail of dust come twisting down the hill like a big brown snake. I yelled at them boys that they was all gonna get in trouble, but they just looked at me like I was something strange, and Bobby whispered real loud to Danny that he better keep me hushed. I stood there trying to think what to do.

Whatever I could of thought of would of been too late anyhow, 'cause it weren't much after that I heard the clatter of the first rock hitting that old black truck. Poor old man. Next thing, them boys come out from behind the bushes, throwing rocks and not even trying to hide. That made it worse, you know, them not even caring if he knowed who they was or not.

I couldn't throw no rocks. Last time we did that, I saw the look on his face. He was worried and mad all right, but there was something else. He had such a sad face! I had sworn I weren't gonna do nothing like that ever again, and now all I could do was wish I weren't there. But I was, and there was that sad face again.

He was so old. But hard to say just how old. His skin was dark brown, like he had been out in the sun a lot, and his long white hair hung down straight and kept getting in his face, so he had to keep brushing it back out of his eyes. He looked me right in the eye when he drove past, and I swear I never seen eyes like he had. They looked like two big black holes in his head. And they was sad, the kind of sad that doesn't cry but just sighs and stays sad.

It was then I knowed. I knowed Be More Happy weren't crazy like they say. He was just a lonely old man. It occurred to me he had good reason to act the way he did, running people off from his place and all. Anybody would run off a bunch of kids they'd seen throwing rocks at them the day before.

I was thinking on that, and watching Be More Happy's old black truck disappear into a cloud of dust, when I noticed them boys was all staring at me. Finally, Freddy Wayne spoke up. He was the oldest, so I reckon he thought it was his duty.

"You done it now, you stupid girl," he snarled. "You let that old man look you right in the eye. You know what that means?" He looked around to make sure he had everyone's attention and then took off his glasses and started polishing the dust off. He always did that when he wanted to look big or important.

"What does it mean?" Danny asked with a shaky voice. Danny is my brother, and he was scared of everything he shouldn't of been scared of. But if it was something he should've had sense enough to be scared of, he weren't.

Jimmy answered for Freddy Wayne. "Means he's done put a hex on your stupid sister!"

"That's twice you boys called her stupid," Junior said without even looking up. He was sitting on the ground, leaning on a big black rock and whittling on a stick. "You don't call no kin of mine stupid, lest you want a busted lip." Junior was my oldest cousin. He always looked out for me and my sister, Lou. I suppose Danny would too, someday, when he was older, but he had a lot of growing to do before he even started to be older. Besides, he was scared. Anytime someone said the word "hex," Danny would get real unnatural quiet and turn kind of white around the mouth. I reckon it had something to do with what goes on at them secret meetings up to them boys' clubhouse.

Bobby and Freddy Wayne and Jimmy was always talking about hexes and drawing funny pictures. Once they spent the whole day drawing pictures in the dirt on the road that went back to Be More Happy's house, and they was so smug that afternoon, telling everyone, "That old man won't be giving us no more trouble," and laughing and hitting each other around. They thought they had fixed him for sure. Well, it rained that night, and you talk about scared boys! They tried not to let on, but not one of them would walk down that road for days. They was afraid they would step in some of that hexed dirt.

Charles Edward and Junior never talked about hexes. They knowed their daddy would skin their backsides if he ever got wind of it. Junior didn't really believe all that, he just thought it was a good joke, but Charles Edward was almost as bad as Danny. He wouldn't come right out and say one way or the other, but he didn't make no jokes about it neither. The funny thing about that is that he is older than Lou. I reckon a person that old ought to know better than believing in hexes. Freddy Wayne knowed better, but he liked to feel superior, like he knowed everything. Like being in the ninth grade weren't enough.

Mama says they make up things like that because there ain't much to do out here in the woods. Seems to me there is plenty to do. But maybe if I was as old as Freddy Wayne, I wouldn't think that. I don't know. But I do know that you can't draw pictures in the dirt or just look at someone and make bad things happen to them. If you could, I'd be looking real hard at some boys right now.

"Let's go on up to the clubhouse," said Jimmy. "Ain't nothing to do around here no more this afternoon." Then he looked directly at me and said, "We need to go work on a hex cure, anyways." Jimmy is Freddy Wayne's little brother. Little if you can call thirteen little. I don't know if he actually believed all that hex mess, but he sure let on he did. And sometimes, when they was talking about it, his eyes got to looking real scared.

Junior said he couldn't go up to the clubhouse. He had to go practice his guitar. And he went on home. Danny looked like he didn't want to go, but I reckon he felt obligated, since I was his sister, and he went on off with the rest of the boys.

That left me alone, but I didn't care. I like to be by myself in the woods. I don't like it when them boys catch crawfish and smush their heads just to get out that pearl. It weren't even really a pearl. Worthless, except for making people sick to their stomachs. But nothing I could ever say stopped them from doing what they wanted. I guess 'cause they was all older than me. But when Lou was there, it was different. They never did things like that when she was around. They all wanted to look good to her. Of course, Charles Edward and Junior were our cousins, but they was the same way. I don't understand it. All she had to do was turn up her nose, or bat her eyelashes, and them boys turned into different people. I could turn green and start to vomit, and they would just laugh and keep right on doing whatever meanness they was up to. Anyways, I just like it better by myself, or else if I have to be with them boys, it's better if Lou is there.

But she weren't always with me. On that particular day, she had gone into town to sing for Johnny Brown, to see if she could be in his show at Boyle Park next Sunday. Wish I could sing or do something. I don't seem to be good for much. I'm not even pretty like her. It's a mystery how two sisters could be so different. Just a little more than a year's difference in our ages, but instead of her being twelve, you'd think she was sixteen or seventeen the way she acts. So ladylike and all with her blond hair and blue eyes, and singing like a bird. Besides that, she always knowed just what to say. Then there's me, with brown hair and brown eyes. Just plain as a potato. And so bashful till it hurts. I always know what to say too, but it just don't come out my mouth. Anyway, none of that would seem so awful if it hadn't been for the fact that everyone was always remarking on the difference between us.

Well, Jimmy was right, they weren't nothing to do. So, I started on home to dig in my garden. Along the way, I saw Mr. Weaver sitting on a stump down by the mailboxes on "H" Street. He took out a big handkerchief and wiped his bald head.

"Heidy, girl," he said.

"Heidy, Mr. Weaver," I said. I don't regularly say "heidy," but I always said it back when Mr. Weaver said it. I bent down and patted old Rex on the head. Hard to say who is older, Mr. Weaver or his old black dog, but I reckon it's Mr. Weaver, were the truth known.

"Saw you'uns throwing rocks at Be More Happy's truck. Ought to be shamed." His voice was real crackly like he had a bad cold. It was always like that.

"I didn't throw no rocks, Mr. Weaver. I use to, but I can't anymore. His eyes look too sad." I was near to crying.

I reckon Mr. Weaver saw that, 'cause he said, "Don't fret, girl. Don't reckon I see too good anymore. But you'd best try to get them boys to be a little nice to that old man. He ain't never done nothing to no one."

Then he looked kind of far away and just sat for a while. I wanted to ask him what he knowed about Be More Happy, but I reckoned it weren't the right time. He didn't look to be in a talking mood.

Finally, he got up, and starting to walk off, he said, "See ya, girl," without even looking at me. Old Rex follered him off down the road. Both of them was so old! And to think, he called Be More Happy a old man. I never knowed anyone as old as Mr. Weaver. But he sure was healthy. He was always going somewhere or coming from somewhere. Even when we went in to town, we'd sometimes see him sitting on a curb resting. No matter how far he was from home, he never would ride when you asked him. He always wanted to walk.

Can't say much for his mind, though. He weren't crazy or nothing like that, but lots of times when I'd see him out walking, I'd ask where he was headed. He'd stop and think for a while, then he'd look behind him at where he come from, and look around like he was lost. Then he'd cough and clear his throat and say where he was going. I knowed he didn't know. He was just walking. And calling me girl. He called all the girls girl, and all the boys boy. The older people he called ma'am or sir. I always figured that was so he wouldn't have to remember all those names. Maybe he was just smarter than the rest of us. I watched him on down the road and then went on home.

I got me the best garden in the whole neighborhood. It may not be as big as some, but there ain't a weed in it, and it's the best spot, just down the hill from the house, past the Indian's grave and right under a pear tree. The whole time I been working it in the spring, that pear tree had been blooming and smelling so sweet it made me want to turn flips.

I sat down on the ground in the hot summer sun and just looked at my garden. They weren't nothing to do. Yesterday, I pulled out the weeds, and I had already watered it that morning. So I just thought. Maybe tomorrow I would go on up to my berry patch and see if they was ripe yet. Spring had been late, but you never could tell about blackberries.

I saw a trail of dust coming toward the house. Maybe that was Mama and Lou. I ran on up and by the time I got there, they was home. Lou was so excited! I knew that meant she'd be singing with Johnny Brown's band on Sunday.

"Did you do it?" I asked. "Did you meet Johnny Brown?"

She had a big grin all over her face and shook her head up and down. "I'm going to sing with him on Sunday!" She was so excited that she was almost in a daze. But her excitement went away when Jimmy come around the corner of the house like he'd been there all along.

"If you don't want nothing to go wrong Sunday, you better stay away from your sister," he said. Then he just stood there looking smug, like he knowed something that the rest of the world didn't.

Lou seemed to have forgotten all about Johnny Brown, and she busied herself with being a big sister. "Annie, what did you do?"

Before I could even start to say anything, Jimmy answered for me. "She just let Be More Happy put a hex on her, that's all. And you ought to know enough about hexes to know to stay away from someone's been hexed." Jimmy's eyes was round with fear. He actually believed that.

"If you think that, what are you doing here in her yard, standing right next to her?" asked Lou.

Jimmy blushed and didn't really want to answer, but made it as good as he could. "'Cause she's my assignment. I have to look after her and make sure nothing bad happens while the others are up to the clubhouse, trying to mix up a hex cure."

"Jimmy, you're just plain dumb," said Lou. Then, like she felt sorry for him, she backed down. "Guess you can't help it, though, being a boy and all." Then as if she had forgotten all about hexes, she asked, "You know where Junior is?"

Jimmy was relieved to have the subject of hexes dropped. He was just like all them other boys. He got all silly around Lou and didn't like to be on her bad side. He told her that he last seen Junior on his front porch playing his guitar and then walked on off into the woods.

Me and Lou went on into the house and had a glass of iced tea. Mama was making fried apple pies, and the whole house smelled like apples and cinnamon. Daddy always said her apple pies is what roped him into marrying Mama. I helped with rolling out the pie crusts while Lou changed into her play clothes. When we were leaving to go on over to Junior's, Mama reminded us to be sure to be home in time to set the table and help with supper.

We hadn't been walking through the woods long before I noticed Jimmy follering us, and I shouted, "You don't stop follering me, Jimmy, I'm gonna share this here gosh-awful hex with you." Then there was a terrible rustling in the bushes behind us and that was the last I seen of Jimmy till later that night with the other boys.

We sat over on Junior's porch singing and fooling around until suppertime. After supper, me and Lou and Danny was all out in the front yard catching lightning bugs when Freddy Wayne, Jimmy, Charles Edward, and Bobby come walking out of the woods. Bobby had a Coke bottle with something in it. He brought it on over and handed it to me.

"The only way you're gonna get rid of that hex Be More Happy put on you is if you drink ever drop of that," said Freddy Wayne, trying hard to keep from laughing right out, while at the same time keeping a safe distance.

"Freddy Wayne, Be More Happy didn't put no hex on me and you know it." I was mad. "Now you go on home before I pour this stinking stuff all over you!" I made like to sling it at him. I could tell by the smell it was water from the branch back by Uncle Ariel's outhouse, and nobody wanted that poured on them. Them boys scattered like the devil was chasing after them.

After they was gone, Danny took the bottle and looked at it like it was some kind of magic. Real scared-like, he asked me, "You not gonna drink it then?"

"There ain't no such thing as a hex, Danny. A person would have to be touched in the head to drink branch water." Then, feeling sorry for him 'cause he really was worried for me, I tried to explain. "Them boys just make up things like that 'cause they like to scare people." But by the look on his face, I knowed he didn't believe me. "Why don't you go on inside and talk to Daddy about it?"

He did. Me and Lou sat out on the front porch listening to the crickets and the whippoorwill. I guess she was thinking about singing with Johnny Brown's band on Sunday. I was thinking about blackberries up on the hill, and about the saddest eyes I ever seen.

Chapter 2

The next morning I was up before Daddy left for work. It was summer again, for sure. I could tell 'cause of the smell of salt mackerel frying for breakfast. Daddy had to eat lots of salt in the summertime 'cause he sweat so much at his work. I always felt sad for Daddy. Seemed to me he never really was happy to go to work, and most times, when he come home he was too tired to be happy about that, too.

That day was gonna be different. Weren't nothing in the world Daddy liked better than fresh blackberry cobbler. And if things worked out right, that's what he'd be having for supper.

I grabbed myself a biscuit with jelly on it and was about to leave, but Mama had different ideas.

"Sit down at the table, Annie. Nobody in this house goes out without a decent breakfast."

I sat down and counted the red squares in the tablecloth while Mama fixed my egg. It would be a waste of good time to argue with her. She always won, and I always ate that egg. And no matter if it was a hundred degrees outside, there was hot chocolate to drink with it. Reckon I was lucky she didn't try putting that salt mackerel down me too.

Finally, I was outside. The other kids was still asleep, but I weren't gonna waste my summer sleeping. Those blackberries were for sure ripe by now.

The birds was really happy that morning. They was all busy, but they took out time to sing. Sometimes, it got downright noisy around there, what with each bird trying to out-sing the other. No matter how hard they all tried, them mockingbirds always won out in the end. Copycats is what they was.

The dirt was still loose in the roads. There weren't even much dew that year. If it didn't start raining soon, everybody's garden was gonna be ruined.

Just then I come to the bridge that crossed the branch by Uncle Ariel's house, and there was Aunt Dorothy out back feeding the chickens. She waved, and I could see her laughing. Guess all her kids was still in bed too. Aunt Dorothy was always so nice, always happy. I reckoned maybe if there was enough berries, I might drop some off by her house on the way home.

I saw something sparkle through the cracks in the old wooden bridge. It was just the sun shining on the water. I laid down flat on the boards and blew the dust away in one spot so I could look down between the cracks. It always looked so cool and shady under there. Sometimes, when it was really hot, I would go underneath and just sit. The fish liked it there, too. I'd have to remember not to tell them boys. They'd be catching the fish just to see them wiggle. They was too little to eat.

Being hot weren't no problem on that day, at least not that early in the morning, so I went on my way up the hill. That was the same hill Be More Happy had been driving down yesterday when he was set on by them boys.

I could smell the kerosene that Mama had soaked my pants legs with. She always did that when I went to pick berries so the chiggers would stay off me. But I always got chiggers anyway. I guess berry picking and kerosene went together just like summer and chiggers.

This berry patch I'm talking about was a really big secret. Them boys spent most of the summer trying to find it, but by being real sneaky, and by going early in the morning, I kept it a secret.

I wasn't mean about it, though. I always shared with the neighbors there about. They was more than enough berries. If them boys had found out where it was, they would've picked all the berries and sold them up at Hillcrest on Saturdays. They was always looking for ways to earn money. Daddy said it weren't right to make money off your neighbors, so I just gave them away.

Anyhow, the berries were right there for anyone to pick. I don't know why nobody else ever found them. They was right there by the spring, up on the "H" Street hill. I been there myself with them boys lots of times. I reckon they just weren't looking for berries at the time.

But somebody did know about my berry patch. I noticed it last summer. I'd have my eye on a couple that was just about ripe and by the time I got back to pick them, they was gone. Never could figure it out. Whoever it was never took much. That led me to believe maybe it was someone like

Mr. Weaver, except I never once saw him up that way. Guess the hill was too high. Besides, he was so slow—walk a little, rest a little, walk a little, rest a little—I knowed if it was him, I'd of seen him sometime.

Then I thought, maybe Doc Elder. But somehow I just couldn't picture that dignified old gentleman with the white beard trudging up a hot dusty hill with a bucket in his hand. Besides, how many times did he say to me, "If I could just get away from this ding-blasted drug store for more than five minutes a day, I'd sit myself down and do some serious fishing." It wasn't Doc Elder.

It could of been Old Man Fox. But I don't reckon. He would be too lazy to go out and get them if they was growing right in his front yard. Everybody else roundabouts had too big a family for a few berries to do any good. I reckon it was just birds.

Just then, I seen something white flash through the bushes on up the hill. I was set to think on that, but a blue jay started diving at my head about then, and I was more interested in getting away from her. Reckon I got too close to her nest. Them jays was downright mean sometimes. Even if they was pretty, they was mean.

Finally, I come to the spring. It was getting to be hot, and my feet was gonna be happy to be in that nice cool water. I rolled up my pants legs and sat down on the ground to put my feet in the water. That was a mistake. Chiggers I could take, but ticks was something else. Right there on my leg was a ugly, creepy, crawly tick. Yuck! I wanted to cry, but that weren't gonna do a whole lot of good. So, I picked up a stick and started trying to scrape it off. Then it was that I got the scare of my life.

I had thought I was alone up there, but a voice come from behind the bushes across from the spring, "You ought to know by now that it's best to get those things off before they bite in."

The worst thing was, it was a voice I never heard before. A deep voice that sounded like it was use to telling people what to do and them doing it. I been playing in those woods all my life, but I never run into no stranger before. While I was trying to figure what to do, he stepped out from behind the bushes. Be More Happy! He weren't smiling or nothing, and he said, "Put down that stick and stop playing with that thing."

I said, "I ain't playing with it. I'm trying to get it off." And my teeth kind of chattered when I said it.

He just stood there, looking in my eyes for a minute, and I could tell he knowed I was scared of it. Then he come over and picked it off my leg, and squishing it between his thumb and fingernails he said, "Little girls who are afraid of ticks ought not go so far back in the woods."

I told him, "I like the woods. I just don't like ticks."

Then there was a long time we didn't say nothing. That was the first time I ever heard Be More Happy talking. First I ever heard of anybody hearing Be More Happy talk. So that was one of the old tales down the drain. Freddy Wayne had been telling people that Be More Happy didn't have no tongue. And then when he was asked what happened to the old man's tongue, he just made a bad face and said, "You don't want to know that." So much for Freddy Wayne.

Then the old man was talking again. "You aren't afraid of meeting up with spooky old men this far back?"

I looked at the old man for a while before answering. He was tall and had muscles just like Daddy, and he wasn't nearly as old as I always thought. He was probably about as old as Granddaddy. But the eyes were the same as I had seen before. And no matter how much them boys say he's a spook, or mean, or weird, I could see by his eyes that he was just lonely.

"You're not spooky, Be More. Everybody says you are, but your eyes don't say it."

"Bemore? Who do you think I am, anyway? Who's Bemore?" He was beginning to sound impatient.

"You are," I said. "Don't you even know what people call you?"

"I've heard those boys calling me things. Things they shouldn't even know about. But I never heard myself called Bemore." He put his big hand over his mouth and kind of squished up his face. I think he was thinking. Then he asked, "Why Bemore?"

"Be More Happy," I said, and his face said he knew why, but I told him anyway. "Your truck. It's painted right acrost the back of your truck. Be More Happy."

He looked like he might smile, but he didn't. Anyhow, he didn't look so worried.

"Nobody knowed your name and everybody knew when we said Be More Happy, we was talking about you. So, that's what we call you." I looked down at the water, embarrassed at talking so much. "You could of told someone your name if you'd cared to."

He looked at me without looking too happy and said, "Oh, sure, I could have introduced myself while you kids were scaring off my chickens, or maybe I could have stopped my truck while it was being pelted with rocks and told everyone what my name was."

He shoved his hands down deep in his pockets and turned to walk away. I didn't say nothing. What could I say? He was right.

He stopped and turned around and looked at me like he just thought of something, and then he asked, "Why didn't you throw any rocks?"

"I couldn't," I said. I could feel tears start to come in my eyes, so I looked down at my feet.

Be More waited for a while, and then he asked very softly, "Why not?"

"I looked in your eyes," I said, careful not to do it again. "All them boys says you're a mean old man, but when I looked in your eyes, you just looked like you was lonely, not mean."

He didn't say nothing, and neither did I. Then he picked a blackberry off the bush and handed it to me. "Berries are good this year." Pointing at my bucket, he said, "Grab your pail there, and I'll help you fill it up."

We started to work filling my bucket with blackberries, and while we was working, we talked a little.

First off he asked me what my name was, then I almost made a bad mistake. I asked him what his name was. I reckon I was asking too much 'cause that sad, lonely look come back over his face, and he waited a long time before he finally answered, "You seem to be comfortable calling me Be More Happy, so let's just keep it that way, okay?"

"Okay," I said. But I was still wondering why he wouldn't tell his name. That made me start to think about some of the things I had heard people saying.

I remember Mama asking Daddy how anyone could live all to themselves like that, and wondering if he was hiding from something. I thought about all the terrible things Freddy Wayne and Jimmy had said about him. Weird. Ghost. Outlaw. Foreigner. But I had always suspected they was just making up those things. Then, just yesterday, what Mr. Weaver had said, "He ain't never done nothing to nobody." And I remembered the way Doc Elder always acted whenever them boys was down to his drugstore talking about Be More and the terrible tricks they had played on him. Doc Elder never said nothing, but he always listened, and he didn't look at all happy about what he was hearing.

Anyhow, it was odd. The two oldest men in these parts seemed to know more about Be More Happy than anyone else, but they wouldn't say nothing. I could tell, though, that they liked him. It was confusing. I didn't believe those things them boys said, but there was no denying, Be More Happy was a mystery.

I watched him picking the berries and once in a while he would look over at me like he knowed exactly what I was thinking. After a little while, he asked, "It really doesn't bother you that your friends say I'm mean or spooky?"

It was like he made all my doubts go away by saying what I was thinking, and I answered, "Don't bother me. They say lots of weird things.

Last summer, my Daddy killed a snake and was letting us feel its skin. Them boys wouldn't get nowhere close. Said snakes don't die till the sun sets."

He just nodded to that. What could anyone say about something that stupid?

After a while, he said, "Well, Annie, I better get on back down the hill. I have a garden to tend." As he was picking a few berries for hisself and wrapping them in his handkerchief, he looked like he was thinking on something. "You ever grow a watermelon? I planted some this year, and there's one in particular that just doesn't seem to want to quit growing. It's a sight!"

Then he waited a while and like he was embarrassed, he said, "If you aren't afraid of spooks or a mean old man, you might stop by my place and see it one of these days."

He still thought I was afraid of him, but I weren't. Not after that morning. I knowed that much for sure. I grinned at him, then I said, "I ain't never seen a watermelon growing. Thanks Be More."

He nodded and had that look of almost smiling on his face when he walked off. A little ways down the hill, he yelled back, "Better get on home with those berries, Annie. And look out for ticks."

I don't even remember walking home. I'd never met anybody like Be More Happy. He weren't at all like them boys said. But how was I gonna convince them of that? They would just think it was the hex working on me.

Chapter 3

I reckon the next couple of days was just like any other day for most everybody else, but they was strange to me. First off, I was surprised 'cause of actually meeting Be More Happy, and then I was anxious to go on over to his house like I said I was gonna do. I don't know nobody that's ever been there before. And the more I thought on it, the more I began to get real nervous and scared-like.

It occurred to me that nobody really knowed a whole lot about Be More except for Doc Elder and Mr. Weaver, and whatever they knowed, they sure kept to themselves.

What with all the mystery about Be More Happy, and me worrying on whether I should go or not, I done something stupid that made things even worse. I told them boys about talking to Be More. I knowed I shouldn't of said nothing, but Freddy Wayne, Jimmy, Bobby, and Charles Edward was all down by the creek laughing and carrying on about how scared Be More was that day they was throwing rocks at his truck. They was making fun of him.

"He didn't yell or nothing like no ordinary human would of done," said Jimmy.

"Told y'all before, he ain't got no tongue," Freddy Wayne said, and he spit on the ground. Then he looked over to me like he was expecting me to get sick or something.

Only I didn't get sick, but I wish now I had. Instead, I had to open up and say something I was sorry for. "Does so, Mr. Smart Mouth! I talked to him myself just day before yesterday. I know he has a tongue. You just been making all that stuff up."

Right about then, all of them boys seemed to lose their tongues and their color, too, except for Freddy Wayne. He was mad, and he always turns red when he gets mad. I don't reckon Jimmy, Bobby, and Charles Edward was mad, though. They was scared. The thought of that old man talking just like a real person had them in a dither, but Freddy Wayne didn't like nobody making him out to be wrong. He was just plain mad.

Charles Edward was the first to speak up. I reckon he was anxious 'cause I was his kin. He kind of laughed like it was all a joke and said, "You don't really mean that now, Annie. Nobody ever talked to that old man long as I knowed about him and that's been all my life." Then when I didn't say nothing, he looked around real sheepish-like and swallowed hard before he asked, "But he didn't actually talk to you, did he?" Charles Edward was as nervous as if I had said I been talking to the old devil.

At last, Freddy Wayne thought up how to take control of the matter and didn't waste any time in doing it. "It's that hex!" he said, a little louder than he needed to. "Y'all know that's what done it." He looked around at the other boys to see what effect that had, and he looked really pleased to see that Jimmy was about scared out of his britches, and poor Bobby was almost as white as his towhead.

I reckon Charles Edward was wishing Junior was there to take over, but he weren't, so it was up to him to try and take up for his rattle-brained cousin this time.

"Don't reckon you ought to be talking like that, Freddy Wayne. Junior says she ain't hexed." I hoped he sounded more convincing to them boys than he did to me.

"Ain't hexed?" Jimmy asked in his high-pitched voice and looked to Bobby and Freddy Wayne for support.

Then Freddy Wayne took up on that. "Ain't hexed? Well, I'm just glad it ain't any of my kin that ain't hexed." Then all three of them started to laughing like that was funny or something and Freddy Wayne said, "You better get your stupid cousin on home, Charles Edward. No telling what kind of meanness that old man will be up to next." He wouldn't of said that if Junior had been there, but he bullied Charles Edward just like everybody else.

Then Freddy Wayne, Jimmy, and Bobby just walked on off and left me and Charles Edward standing there. After looking at me like I was a puzzlement that he really didn't want to think on, he finally said, "Come on, Annie, I'll walk you on over to your house."

"No!" I said. "I ain't scared to walk myself home. Be More Happy ain't gonna hurt nobody."

I never seen a person look more relieved than Charles Edward did just then. "Okay, then," he said, "but you go straight home." And he run off in the direction that them other three had just done.

Wonder what he would of said if I'd told him I weren't going home but over to Be More Happy's house. He'd probably have just run a little faster.

I sat down on the little bridge crossing the creek to think for a while. That was my favorite thinking spot and the reason I had come down to the creek in the first place. I knowed them boys was wrong about Be More, but I was still scared to go on over to his house. It was so far back in the brush. Actually, it weren't that far, it was right there at the foot of the Hayes Street hill on "H" Street, but it was so overgrowed no one could see it from the road. Sometimes, when you was passing by at night, you could see a light through the bushes, but that just made it scarier.

After a while, I got up on my feet and headed on over there. I told him I'd come, didn't I? That didn't keep me from hoping I'd meet Mr. Weaver or someone along the way to slow me down some.

No such luck. I come up to Be More Happy's house from the woods at the back, and my first regret was that I hadn't come by way of the road. There I was, right in the middle of them woods, close enough I could see Be More's house through the trees, and hearing some awful strange sounds. I heard footsteps crackling over dead leaves, and then something being drug through the woods. I wasn't too sure that I wanted to know who was dragging what, so I hid behind a big oak tree and started sweating like a washwoman. What if all the things them boys had said were true? What if this place really was haunted? Maybe it was Be More Happy's ghost I met up in them woods, and he tricked me into coming to this place. Then I heard them chickens squawking like they was getting killed. Chickens don't squawk like that for no good reason.

I was looking around the tree to see if the coast was clear so I could get out of there when I heard a familiar sound. There was a long drawn-out sniffle. A sniffle I had been hearing since I was old enough to know what a sniffle was. That was Jimmy's runny nose if I ever heard it! His mama calls it his sinus condition, but to me it was just a plain runny nose. There it went again. But what was Jimmy doing back here by Be More Happy's place? He was scared to death of that old man. Unless ...

Then it was I heard the snickering and the sound of running feet. Not just Jimmy, either! I stepped out from behind the tree, and as it would happen, I stepped right in front of Freddy Wayne and scared him so bad he let out a yelp that stopped the other boys dead in their tracks.

I never saw nothing so funny. I seen Jimmy and Bobby and Charles Edward scared before, but I never seen Freddy Wayne scared. He was always the one doing the scaring, but this time it was him that was scared. His eyes was bugged out so far they was practically touching his eye glasses.

I knowed I was in trouble then, 'cause as soon as he seen they weren't nothing to be scared of, he was sure to be mad.

By then, I had figgered out what they had been up to, and I was as mad as Freddy Wayne was. I yelled at them, "I'm gonna tell all your mamas what you been doing! Don't you have no shame?"

Freddy Wayne had pulled hisself together and he was mad, just like I thought. "You ain't gonna tell nobody nothing," he said in a low voice with his teeth gritted together. Then he put both hands on his hips, and stretching hisself out to be as tall as he could, he leaned way over me and shouted, "What you doing follering us around in the woods anyhow?"

I weren't gonna take that from nobody. I stretched myself up trying to be just as tall, and hollered right back at him, "I weren't follering nobody! I come to see Be More Happy!"

That left him as speechless as the other boys had been. So while they was all wondering what to say next, I started on through the woods to Be More's house.

Bobby was the first one to move. He run up behind me and grabbed my arm. "Annie, what do you think you're doing? You can't go down there." His voice was strange, like he was about to cry. When he seen I was ignoring him, he tried again. "Not now, Annie. We was just scaring off his chickens, and that old man is gonna be mad."

Then Jimmy hollered to me from where he was. He didn't want to get no closer to that house. "He's gonna think you was helping us!" And then he sniffled real loud.

I looked back, half-wondering if they was right, and thinking maybe I better wait and go some other day. But Freddy Wayne was standing there with that smug look on his face. "She ain't going nowhere," he said. Then he just stood there with his hands on his hips like he was daring me to take another step. So I did just that. Even if I knowed there was a ghost waiting there to chew off my head, I'd of gone, just to show them boys I weren't scared.

When I got about halfway down to Be More's place, Charles Edward yelled, "You go any closer, Annie, and I'm gonna tell your mama!"

"You do, and I'll tell your mama you was scaring off Be More Happy's chickens!" I hollered back, and just kept right on walking.

Then Bobby called to me again, "Annie, come on back, we was just teasing you." Bobby was just as mean as all them other boys till it come right down to the nitty-gritty, then he couldn't stand it if he thought someone was gonna get hurt.

I just kept on like I didn't hear nothing, but I did hear them boys running off through the woods.

On my way down to the house, I seen where they had dropped the gate to Be More's chicken yard and picked it up.

When I got to his place, Be More was out back gathering up his chickens. He had a hold of four chickens by their feet and looked up real mean at me. Finally I said, "I brought back your gate."

He hadn't moved a inch. The chickens was fluttering around, trying to get out of his hands. Then he said, in a not too happy voice, "You were in on this?"

I shook my head no. I was ashamed that it even looked that way.

He stood there a minute longer, and then, nodding over to the chicken yard, he said, "If you'll stand that gate up over there where it goes, I'll put these chickens back in their pen."

I stood the gate up where it belonged. Then, gathering up the rest of the chickens, I threw them over the fence while Be More wired the gate back in place.

Be More's house was old. It was big, too. Big enough for two or three families. It almost reminded me of a castle, only it was made of wood. Wood that weren't painted. The windows was all up high, close to the roof, and went all the way around the house. Guess he didn't want no one looking in. But the strangest part was, it weren't built on the ground. It was standing up on poles that looked like stilts.

I reckon I shouldn't of stared the way I did, 'cause Be More noticed right off and started to explain. "Used to flood out here before they graded Hayes Street and put in those big ditches. My father had the house built up like that after his first house got washed away in a spring flood."

That didn't make sense to me, and I asked. "Why didn't he just build it on up the hill a ways?"

Be More looked at the house, and then up the hill, then back to the house again. "Never said. Come to think of it, I never asked." Then he laughed. It started out soft but before he was finished, he was really laughing. It was strange but nice.

We talked on for a while about floods and gardens and things, but he never did say why the windows was up so high. He showed me the watermelon I had come to see. It was huge, and looking to get even bigger. I wish Daddy had planted watermelon.

When we come back up to the house from the garden, Be More had me to sit down on a bench that went all the way around a big oak tree in his back yard, and he went inside for a minute. I looked around at the yard and house. Even though the house was strange, it was neat. The yard was neat, too. It weren't no more than a big clearing in the brush that grew up all around it. Nothing fancy about it, but it was neat.

Be More come out his back door carrying two Mason's root beers. "Would you care for a root beer, Annie?"

"Thanks," I said. I reckon he knowed how much kids love root beer.

He said, "I don't know of anything better than a nice cold root beer on a hot summer day." He was smiling again and it gave me a real good feeling inside. But seeing him smile made me think about them boys being so mean, and I decided to see what I could do about that.

"Be More," I said, "them boys wouldn't be playing such mean tricks on you if they knowed you better."

His face wasn't smiling anymore. He just looked off into the woods. Then I went on. "They aren't really bad. They just think you are strange 'cause you don't never talk to nobody, and you live here all by yourself." His eyes was dark and sad again, and I felt real bad about what I had said. I wished I had just kept quiet.

Finally, after not saying nothing for a long time, he said in a mean voice, "I don't need to know anyone. I don't need anybody nosing into my business." It was like he was talking to hisself, but I reckoned he meant me, and I figured it was time for me to go on home. I got up and set the empty bottle on the bench. He was still staring off into the woods.

"Thanks for the root beer, Be More," I said. "I reckon I better be getting on home."

Then he looked at me like he was coming out of a trance. "What's that?" he said in a softer voice. "You have to leave so soon, Annie?"

"Reckon I better," I said. He knowed I was upset.

"Annie," he said. "I didn't mean you were being nosy. I guess it's been so long since I talked to anyone, I have forgotten how to do it."

"That's all right, Be More." I didn't like to make him sad, so I was gonna have to be real careful about what I said from now on.

When I looked at him, he was looking at me with those big sad eyes again. "Annie, I want you to know that you are the first person to come to this house since I moved in twenty-one years ago." He was staring off into the woods again. "You are the first person I have even spoken to in all these years." He thought for a while, and then said, "I never meant for it to be that way."

I didn't say nothing, and after a while he turned back to me and I could see he was smiling again. "Promise me, Annie. Promise me you'll come back and see me." He was talking like he really meant it.

I was still curious about a lot of things, but I reckoned that weren't the time to be asking a lot of questions, so I just said, "Sure, Be More, I'll be back.

But I reckon I better go for now. Thanks for the root beer."

"You're welcome, Annie. Anytime." He was looking sad again. I couldn't understand all the changes.

Walking on into the woods, I hollered back, "See you, Be More."

And he would be seeing me! Maybe more than he wanted to. I never seen nobody so much in need of a friend. And somehow, I was gonna have to get them boys to thinking better of him. He could use more than one friend, whether he knowed it or not.

I had a lot to think on, but the main thing right then was getting home fast as I could. I'd be getting the switch if I weren't home in time to help with fixing supper.

Chapter 4

I seen it coming just as plain as I seen the sun go down not fifteen minutes ago. Danny dropped the spoon in the gravy bowl. There ain't nothing makes Daddy madder than having to fish a spoon out of a gravy bowl. But Danny was smart this time. He weren't about to get into trouble again after getting his breeches burned last night for shooting a robin with his BB gun.

"Guess where Annie went today," he said, thinking to save his skin. But then, he swallowed hard 'cause no one was trying to guess, and Daddy was looking real hard at the gravy bowl. Then, just when Daddy was getting ready to say something about the spoon not being in the gravy, Danny almost shouted out, "That old man's house!" And seeing that he had Daddy's attention, he went on to tell it all. "Annie went down to Be More Happy's house."

Daddy's eyes was on me, expecting me to say I didn't do it. But I just reached for another biscuit and acted like I didn't hear what Danny said.

I tried to keep my head down, but I couldn't help noticing that things was getting real unnatural quiet. So I looked up, and just like I thought, everyone was staring at me. Everyone but Lou, and she was looking at Danny like she'd like to wring his neck. Mama had a worried expression on her face, but not Daddy. His jaw was twitching like it always does when he's mad. Finally, he said, "You been down to that old man's house?"

I nodded yes, and looked down at my plate. Everything was quiet again, but it didn't last long. Daddy said, "Reckon you better explain yourself, Annie." He was fishing for the spoon in the gravy bowl. "Start at the beginning, and let's hear it all."

So I started at the beginning. I told about meeting Be More Happy up by the spring when I was picking blackberries, and I noticed the surprised look on Mama's face when I said that we talked. I told about him asking me to come by and see his watermelon, and about them boys throwing rocks and scaring off Be More's chickens. I told about Be More's house and how neat everything was back behind all that brush. And about his eyes, how lonely they look. Not mean, just lonesome. Finally, I come back to the watermelon. I thought Daddy would like that.

"You have to see that watermelon, Daddy. I never seen one growing before, and Be More says it's a really big one."

Daddy was thoughtful and not nearly so mad. He looked to Mama and asked, "You know anything about that old man, Hon?"

Mama's face was sad when she answered, "That old house has been down there for as long as I know. Since before I was born, I reckon. We use to play down there in the summer. Like Annie said, the windows are all up high, so I never saw inside, and the doors was always locked tight.

"The place was a real mystery to us kids. Then one day we went down there to play, and the garage door was standing wide open with the old black truck sitting out front. The old man was working on it, and when he heard us come up, he just stood there and stared." Mama shuddered and then went on. "It was weird. Nobody knowed who he was or where he come from. But Doc Elder kept saying for us to let him be, like he knowed something but weren't gonna say. After a while, we got use to him being around. Only time anyone ever saw him was coming and going in that old black truck of his. I heard a lot of stories. Probably same ones still being told today. The only one I ever believed, though, was that he couldn't talk." She looked over to me and asked, "Annie, are you sure? He talked to you? It weren't just you talking and him listening?"

"I'm sure, Mama," I said.

Everyone had finished eating, and Danny asked to be excused but weren't answered. Daddy was talking to Mama. "You reckon we ought to keep tighter reins on some of these kids? No telling about that old man."

Mama looked at me and thought for a while. First off, there was worry lines on her face, but when she answered Daddy, it weren't worried but proud, she was. "Annie knows more about these woods and the people in them than anyone I know. You can't keep a kid in a box. Be More Happy hasn't never hurt no one around here. Don't reckon he's gonna change his ways this late in life." Then she said something I didn't understand, but it seemed to be the answer Daddy was waiting for. She looked at him like they had a secret, and said, "And a little child shall lead them." And they walked out into the front room.

As soon as they was out of sight, Danny got up from the table and said in a mimicking voice, "Why sure, Danny. You may be excused. And thank you for telling us about your stupid sister …"

"Thank you?" Lou hissed. "You know you did that just to save your own skin."

Danny laughed, prissy like a girl. "Worked, too, didn't it?"

Lou and me turned our backs and left him laughing. Then he stopped and got real serious. I could tell he was thinking about all that was said at supper. "You know you're getting into real trouble, don't you, Annie? You just wait and see what Freddy Wayne has to say about all this!"

I just looked at him with the meanest look I had and didn't say nothing.

"Don't you never listen?" He was getting excited again, and his face was almost as red as his hair. "Freddy Wayne knows all about that old man, and you heard all the tales he tells." Then a look come acrost his face that give me the cold shivers. "It's that hex. It is!" His mouth was still hanging open when he finally left the kitchen. I never seen no one could scare their own self as good as Danny could.

Me and Lou cleaned up the kitchen, and while we was working, she practiced the new song she was learning for Sunday afternoon. We was right there in the kitchen, but in our minds, she was at Boyle Park and I was up on the hill at them boys' clubhouse. It was always like that, we was together, but then again, we wasn't.

Finally, when we finished, she leaned against the cabinet and asked, "Annie, are you sure you should be hanging around that spooky old man?"

"He ain't spooky," I said. "He's just as nice as anyone. Nicer than most."

She held up her hands like she was surrendering some big battle or something. "Okay. Okay. Mama seems to think you know what you're doing. It just seems weird to me." She looked at me with her little pout. "He ain't never talked to no one all this time, but then he runs across a little freckly-faced girl out in the woods and starts being real sociable. Don't make sense to me."

I weren't sure, but I got the feeling she was upset 'cause it weren't her he decided to open up to.

Just then, Mama called out from the front room that *Fibber McGee and Molly* was on. Lou went on out, and I finished washing off the stove.

When I went out, everything seemed to be back to normal. The whole family was sitting around the radio. Mama was sewing a dress for Lou to wear Sunday, Lou and Danny were sitting on the rug in front of the radio, and Daddy was reading the paper. I won't never understand how he does that! He reads and listens to the radio at the same time. That don't appear to me to be too easy a thing to do, but that's my daddy. He always has two or three irons in the fire.

During the commercial, Daddy said something that made all of us lose interest in Fibber McGee. "I hear the Smiths are getting a television."

"So is Brother," Mama said. "Brother" is Uncle Ariel. Mama never growed out of calling him that.

Was they thinking about getting one? All three of us kids sat there waiting, scared if we moved we'd miss what was about to be said.

"Reckon we could go down to Cox's on Saturday and look at some," Daddy said in his own good time. "On Friday nights there's boxing. That'd be worth it all, right there."

Mama stopped her sewing and looked out the window like she was thinking on something real hard, and then she said, "Boxing in our own front room? That don't hardly seem decent."

Danny took it on hisself to fill in the quiet that followed what Mama said. I ain't about to try and tell what all he had to say on the subject of television. It was mostly begging anyhow.

Lou's eyes was shining, and her face said she was miles away. If I knowed her any at all, she was dreaming about singing on the television.

I weren't all that concerned one way or the other. It'd be nice, but the radio weren't all that bad. I wondered if Daddy could read while he watched the television.

All of a sudden there was a gosh-awful sound coming from the radio that set my teeth on edge. I knowed it was coming. It came on ever week at that time, but it still scared me. *The Screeching Door!*

Scared ain't exactly the word you'd use to describe Danny, though. He was pale as a ghost. Even though he weren't never allowed to listen to it all the way through, that first screech was enough to scare the pants off him.

Daddy was trying hard not to laugh right out. He said to Danny, "That's enough for you, young man. Get on off to bed. You don't need nothing else to scare you. I'm tired of sleeping three to a bed," and he winked at Mama. They was always winking to each other when they said something they thought nobody else knowed nothing about. But I reckon we all knowed a little more than they thought.

After that program was over, me and Lou went to bed, too. We talked for a long, long time. It was too hot to sleep anyhow. They weren't even no breeze, but it was nice. I could hear the whippoorwills and frogs, and sometimes even a coyote. I'd much rather be hot than cold, and in the winter it was colder than it was hot in the summer.

I listened while Lou told me for the fifteenth time every detail of her meeting with Johnny Brown. How handsome he was. What a really good singer he was. How nice. How this. How that. Was she ever gonna quit so I cold talk?

Finally! I reckon it was the coyote hollering up on the hill that stopped her. She never was crazy about wild things. She weren't scared, least she didn't let on if she was. She just didn't like them.

I took advantage of the pause and changed the subject. "Know what I'm gonna do tomorrow?" I asked.

She sighed, like she already knowed what I was gonna say. "You aren't going back to that old man's house are you, Annie?"

I just couldn't understand how everyone could be so turned against someone they didn't even know. "I reckon I might, if I want to!" I said. "But that weren't what I was gonna say. I'm going up to them boys' clubhouse. I'm gonna ask them to be nicer to Be More. Maybe if I tell them how nice he is, and that he's lonely, they'll understand."

"You're crazy. You know that, don't you?" Lou was sitting up in bed now. She weren't scared like Danny would of been. Just mad. Well, maybe more worried than mad. "Girls aren't allowed up there. Remember what they said would happen to any girls they caught snooping around?" She was whispering through her teeth so it sounded like she was hissing. "They said they'd take her inside, take all her clothes off, and then send her home *naked*!"

"That's hogwash and you know it," I said. "You know Freddy Wayne. He's the one told everyone that Be More Happy didn't have no tongue, and I know better than that."

"You're right about one thing. I know Freddy Wayne! I know things I never told you about. Bad things. And them boys will do anything he says." She was worried all right. I stopped to think for a while. She was right, Freddy Wayne was mean, but maybe ... "Maybe Junior will be there. Freddy Wayne won't start nothing with Junior around." I was sure I had found the solution to all my problems. But Lou weren't so sure.

"That's a awful big maybe. Junior don't hang around with them boys much anymore. He mostly sits over on his front porch playing his guitar. He's getting pretty good, too." I could tell by her voice she had quit thinking about Freddy Wayne and was dreaming about singing again.

If Lou didn't make it as a big country singer, it wouldn't be for lack of dreaming. That's all she ever talked about. First off, she was to get on the Barnyard Frolics, and she done that last year. Since then she's been singing at the parks on Sunday, whenever she gets a chance, and the Barnyard Frolics on Saturday nights. Her next big step was gonna be the

Louisiana Hayride, and after that, the Grand Ole Opry. And who knows where from there?

I had heard that dream so many times, sometimes I didn't know if it was hers or mine. But it was hers all right. I couldn't carry a tune in a bucket. And it was for sure if I had to get up and sing in front of all them people, I'd wet my pants. No, she could have her dream, and I'd be content to have the kids pointing at me at school 'cause I was her sister.

I just wish Lou hadn't reminded me about what Freddy Wayne said. I ain't never heard of them doing nothing like that, but I ain't never heard of no girls going up there before either.

"Ouch!" I felt a sharp elbow in my ribs.

"I asked you about my hair," Lou said. "Do you think I should wear it in pigtails?" Then she went on talking, without even waiting for my answer. "I wore it that way at the Barnyard Frolics last week but, I'm not sure …" and on and on she went.

If she'd waited, I'd of told her I don't like it that way. Only time she ever wears pigtails is when she's singing at one of them shows. It's like saying she's something she's not. We ain't really all that country. We're just plain people. Besides, she's got pretty hair, and pigtails don't do nothing but frizz it up.

Guess it was what Lou said, and the fact that it was so blooming hot that night, that made me have awful dreams. I dreamed I was up to the clubhouse and Junior weren't there, and them boys was about to do just what Freddy Wayne had said they would do. But before they got a chance, a ghost walked through the wall of the clubhouse and scared them all off. A ghost with big black eyes and long white hair. He stood there in the door to the clubhouse laughing after them boys running down the hill. Only it weren't a happy laugh. It was scary, and I ran off, too.

When I woke up I was mad at myself. I guess I was really still scared of Be More, no matter what I said to other people. Inside, I was still scared.

Chapter 5

The next morning started out to be beautiful. I wish it had stayed that way.

I got up soon as I heard Mama banging things around in the kitchen and was in time to eat breakfast with Daddy. He was in a good mood. That surprised me after last night. I never did decide if I was in trouble or not.

While Daddy was shaving, I ran on out the backdoor without even saying bye to Mama. Didn't do me no good, though. First thing I knowed, Daddy was stopped beside me on the road, asking if I wanted to ride. Reckon if I'd thought about it, I would of took the path through the woods. But I weren't thinking about nothing but getting up to that clubhouse before any of them boys. I knowed if I heard them up there, I'd back down. I knowed that for sure.

"Where you headed for, Annie?" Daddy asked.

"Just over the hill," I said. And then I decided I better tell it all. "I'm going up to them boys' clubhouse."

I opened the door and got in the car like Daddy said. I was surprised when he didn't argue, didn't try to tell me how dangerous it was to go up to that clubhouse. Maybe he didn't know. When he stopped at the foot of the hill to let me out, he said, "You take care of yourself, Annie." Then he winked real big. I didn't understand. I'll never understand parents. I guessed it had something to do with what Mama said last night about a little child being the leader. But heck, I ain't no leader. I ain't even a very good follower.

Anyhow, it was good to know Daddy weren't mad at me, whatever the reason was. I said, "I'll take care, Daddy." And the next minute I was standing alone in the middle of the road, watching our old car disappear into a cloud of dust. Alone! I don't think I was that nervous the time I went down to Be More's house. I started on through the woods. Scared or not, it had to be done.

I hadn't gone into that part of the woods in a long time, and it seemed strange to me, almost spooky. Them boys hadn't allowed no one anywhere near since they built that clubhouse. But thanks to Danny and his waggly tongue, I knowed exactly where it was, and that's where I went.

Yuck! You couldn't call it a pretty place. It was made out of old scraps of lumber and whatever else they could nail together. I couldn't even tell you exactly what shape it was. Just ugly. In fact, it was so ugly it almost made the whole place look bad. And it ain't easy to make these woods look bad.

The only window was up too high for me to see in, and there was an old piece of burlap nailed up over the door. I didn't go in right off. Most times I ain't scared of things like that, but after what Lou said, and that dream I had last night, I weren't too eager to go inside.

I looked around real careful-like. I don't know what I was looking for—most likely a way to get out fast if I needed to. Even though my good sense told me to stay out, I went on inside. It was dark and damp. The only light come from that one little window. Soon as my eyes got use to the dark, I was sorry I didn't stay outside.

What a mess. Them boys ain't nothing but pigs, and there I stood right in the middle of their waller. There was an old box turned upside down right in the middle of the floor. I reckon it was supposed to be a table. And sitting right on top of a bunch of papers was a half burned candle and a box of matches. That right there was enough to keep Danny in the yard for the next month. There was empty sardine cans, Coke bottles, comic books, and all kinds of paper scattered all over the place. There was also a smell that smelled kind of like an old ashtray.

Then it was I knowed why they didn't want no one around. I just been there a minute, and already knew enough to get ever last one of them in trouble. It weren't only the cigarettes or the matches, either. Those papers on the floor had pictures drawed on them that was really bad. There was one had a picture of a lady without no clothes on.

Just then, I heard a sound outside. Someone was coming! They was too close for me to run. I looked around for a place to hide, but they weren't no place. So, I just stood there and gritted my teeth. I saw the burlap door being pulled back and, thank goodness, Bobby's white head ducking through the door. I weren't nearly so scared of him as I was of Freddy Wayne and Jimmy. Bobby had a good streak in him. Freddy Wayne and Jimmy was just plain mean.

He didn't notice me right off, but soon as he struck that match to light the candle, he seen me standing there. Scared him more than it did me. He dropped the match and said something he shouldn't of said, and then he became more worried than scared.

"Annie! What are you doing here?" He was looking at the door behind him. Then he grabbed my arm and started dragging me out. "Freddy Wayne is on his way up here right now. Are you crazy?" All of a sudden the curtain over the door was drawed back. Bobby's face turned pure white, and he pushed me into the corner and stood in front of me. When he started to breathe again, he sighed, "Charles Edward."

"Who's that you're hiding in the corner, Bobby?" he asked with a big grin on his face. But when Bobby stepped aside, and Charles Edward seen it was me, the grin disappeared fast.

"We gotta get her out before Freddy Wayne and Jimmy get up here," Bobby said, almost pleading.

"I ain't going nowhere," I said. My courage had come back when I seen how scared they was. "I come up here to talk some sense into you boys' heads, and I'm gonna do it!"

Bobby looked like he was gonna cry, but Charles Edward was mad. "What you come for is to get yourself in a whole lot of trouble!" he said as he grabbed me and started trying to push me out the door. "Why can't you be normal like Lou? Why do you always have to make me look bad?"

We stopped fussing when we both noticed Bobby had gone completely white again. I turned around to see what had scared him, and there was Freddy Wayne's face in the window.

He had the same kind of look on his face that he got when he caught a grasshopper, or a bird, or something that he didn't have no good intentions about. And I reckon I didn't feel any better than those creatures must feel when they was caught by a mean one like Freddy Wayne.

Jimmy had come on inside and was strutting around like a banty rooster, saying all sorts of mean things about what ought to be done. He didn't scare me none, though. I expected all of them to act just the way they did. All but Bobby and Freddy Wayne.

Bobby surprised me because he was truly worried. He acted the way I would of expected Lou to, and the way Charles Edward should have.

But the thing that worried me most was Freddy Wayne. He weren't acting like hisself at all. He just grinned and didn't say nothing. Soon as Jimmy started to slow down a little bit, Freddy Wayne come on in and sat down behind the table. He banged a rock on a board and said, "This here special meeting is now in session."

Then Bobby stepped in front of me and said, "You can't have no special meeting, Freddy Wayne. All the members ain't here."

Jimmy sniffed his nose real loud and said, "Close enough. Only one ain't here is Junior, and he don't hardly ever come no more."

"What about Billy and Jerry?" Bobby asked.

"Billy and Jerry is still in California. Won't be here till next week," Freddy Wayne said, and squinted his eyes at Bobby. "Why is it you ain't wanting this meeting, Bobby? You ain't scared, are you?"

If it's possible, Bobby turned even whiter than he already was and said, "I ain't scared, but rules is rules."

Charles Edward hadn't said nothing, hadn't moved, but I could feel his wishing he weren't there.

"Let's get on with this meeting," Freddy Wayne said, and grinned at me again. "Now, Bobby here has just reminded us all that rules is rules. It seems to me I remember a rule about girls in this here clubhouse. Anyone remember that rule?" He looked in all their faces.

The only sound was that loud sniffle that always come before Jimmy said anything, and sure enough, "We all know the rule, Freddy Wayne." Then he started to giggle. Jimmy giggled just like a girl.

Freddy Wayne looked at Bobby and Charles Edward, and said, "Seeing as how we all remember the rules, I guess we better get on with the enforcing of them," and he stood up.

"You lay a hand on me, Freddy Wayne, and you gonna be in more trouble than you ever dreamed about!" I was talking brave, but all the while I was backing away from that strange, quiet Freddy Wayne.

"We got rules about girls in our clubhouse, and you're just about to find out all about them," Freddy Wayne said as he continued to come at me real slow-like.

I heard Jimmy giggling back behind him and saw the scared look on Charles Edward's face. Out of the corner of my eye, I seen Bobby bend down and pick something up off the floor, and then the whole clubhouse seemed to be a cloud of feet, arms, dust, and dirty words.

Let me tell you, I didn't waste no time getting out that door. Just when I thought I was clear of the place, I run flat into someone. Junior! I never in my life been so glad to see no one.

Right on my heels, coming out the door was Freddy Wayne, and then Jimmy. They stood speechless for a while, like a cat that was caught with feathers all over its mouth. Then Bobby and Charles Edward come out. I never saw no one look more relieved than Charles Edward did. Bobby was different, though. He weren't scared white no more. Matter of fact, his face was red like he was mad. Don't know what he was mad about.

"Somebody gonna tell me what's going on up here?" Junior come over to me and put his arm around my shoulder. "You okay, Annie?"

I nodded my head, yes. I weren't sure if I could talk or not.

Freddy Wayne said, "You know the rules, Junior. No girls."

"I know the rules, Freddy Wayne. Reckon stupid rules is meant to be broke." He looked real hard at Freddy Wayne. "What do you reckon?"

Then Freddy Wayne said a word I ain't about to tell you, and quicker than lightning, Junior reached out and socked him right on the mouth. Give him a busted lip!

Freddy Wayne looked like he wanted to hit back, but he didn't. If the truth was known, Freddy Wayne was one of the biggest cowards roundabouts. That's probably why he was so mean.

Junior was still standing there with his arm around my shoulder, as calm as if he had just swatted a fly. "Now, since things is quieted down some," he said directly to Freddy Wayne, "let's hear what Annie has to say." His hand tightened on my shoulder and he said, "Go ahead, Sugar, say what you come up here to say."

I didn't really want to talk. It all seemed so stupid after all that happened. Them boys was mad, and mad people don't listen. But I was mad, too, and I weren't gonna take all I'd taken that morning for nothing.

"I just come up here to tell you boys you're wrong about Be More Happy," I said softly. "All them stories about him is just made up. He ain't no ghost and he ain't mean. He's lonely." I looked in their faces and didn't see nothing. Like I thought, they wasn't even listening, but I couldn't stop myself from saying what I had to say.

"You ought to be shamed about all the tricks and mean things you done. It'd be just the same if someone throwed rocks at your own grandpas. Only, they could go on home to their families and get comforted. Be More ain't got nobody." They weren't listening! "He's just lonely." I was wasting my breath. "He's nice. He's really a nice old man."

What was the use? If I'd told them he was from Mars, they would of listened and been thrilled to hear it.

Freddy Wayne mumbled something under his breath and went on down the hill with Jimmy follering not far behind. Charles Edward looked at Junior like as if to say, "What now?" and Junior patted me on the shoulder.

"You can't change people's ideas overnight, Annie," he said. "They'll come around. Now, tell me what happened before I got here."

"Nothing happened," Charles Edward answered nervously. "Freddy Wayne called a special meeting, and said that the rules had to be enforced. He was about to try to enforce them hisself. While I was trying to figure what to do, Bobby pulled that old rug out from under everybody's feet. That's when Annie run out the door."

"You did that, Bobby?" Junior laughed. "I'd like to seen that!"

"Lucky you come when you did," Bobby said. "I ain't never seen Freddy Wayne so mad." He was turning a rock over with his bare foot. It was clear he didn't want to talk about it. "Reckon I'll get on home. Charles Edward, want to come over to my house?"

They started on down the hill the same way Freddy Wayne and Jimmy had gone. Weren't but one path down the hill.

"I'll walk you on over to your place, Annie," Junior said. "You best stay clear of Freddy Wayne and Jimmy for a while."

I had to ask, even though I was sure I already knew the answer. "How come you to come up to the clubhouse this morning, Junior?"

"Lou called to tell me what you was up to, and asked if I'd come up and check on you," he said.

We walked on for a ways without talking. I was embarrassed 'cause of having to be took care of like I was a baby. Didn't do no good, neither. I really messed things up that day. Them boys would probably be twice as mean to Be More now.

"You really talk to that old man, Annie?" Junior asked.

"Really did," I said. "And he talked to me, too." I picked a handful of honeysuckle and started to suck the nectar off them. "Guess I kind of messed things up today, huh?"

Junior didn't answer right off. He was thinking. Finally, almost half way home, he said, "Can't never tell. You just can't never tell."

Chapter 6

Do I have to tell you that I stuck close to home for the next few days? Mama thought I was coming down with something. Lou didn't never mention it, one way or the other. But I reckoned it was a dumb thing I did, and I felt bad about it. Them boys could have their old clubhouse and welcome to it.

On Thursdays, I had to walk up to the catholic school with Lou for her piano lesson. It weren't a bad walk, just past Doc Elder's place, and best of all was the soda we stopped to get on the way back home. Well, it was Thursday and there we sat at the soda fountain in Doc Elder's drugstore.

Doc Elder was one of my favorite people. He was old, but he weren't bent, and he weren't mean. He looked like someone out of a storybook with his twinkly eyes and his white bushy beard. I reckon one of the reasons everybody liked Doc Elder so much was 'cause of what he was doing right now, which was listening. Lou could talk the horns off a billy goat when it come to her singing, but Doc Elder just smiled like he enjoyed all her jabber.

She was telling him about Johnny Brown and the show last Sunday, when Jimmy, Bobby, Charles Edward, and Freddy Wayne come in and was picking drinks out of the pop box. Doc Elder politely excused himself and went over to help the boys. So while I finished my soda, I got the leftovers of everything I been hearing since Sunday in one ear and heard them boys saying something about Billy and Jerry in the other ear.

As it happened, it didn't matter that I couldn't hear what they was saying 'cause soon as the little bell jingled on the door, I turned around and seen who was coming in. Sure enough, it was Billy and Jerry, back to spend some time with Granny.

Billy and Jerry was orphans, and they spent all their time going from relative to relative, but mostly they stayed with Granny. And Granny most times called them Pete and Repeat. Every time you seen one, you seen the other. Only time I ever seen them apart was when they was in school, and that was only 'cause Billy was in the sixth grade and Jerry in the fourth.

Billy was a big boy with dark hair and dark eyes, but Jerry was a regular little squirt. He was blond and blue eyed, my age, but almost half my size.

They was all talking, hitting each other around, and acting crazy. After a while, they started making all their plans for the summer, and Billy said, "We got this really neat trick for that old guy down by the creek. You're gonna love it."

Right about then, you could of heard a pin drop in that place. Everybody was looking at each other real uncomfortable-like.

Billy was the one broke the silence. "What's wrong?" he said. "What'd I say?"

"Nothing," Freddy Wayne answered. Then he turned his pop bottle up, emptying it in one swallow, and slammed the empty bottle into the rack. "You didn't do nothing," he said, and looked at me real hateful. "Let's get on out of here."

They went out a lot quieter than they come in. Soon as the door closed behind them, Doc Elder started asking questions.

"Either of you girls know what that was all about?"

"We know," Lou said. "I thought by now the whole world would know."

"Everything that goes on in these parts, sooner or later, makes its way across this counter," Doc Elder said as he started to clean up. "Go ahead and tell. What's this got to do with …"—He paused for a minute like he almost said something he shouldn't and then finished—"Be More Happy?"

"It's Annie, Doc," Lou said. "She met Be More Happy out in the woods and says he talked to her. Then she went over to his place for a visit and it's got them boys all riled up."

I mean to tell you, I never seen Doc Elder speechless, but he was just then. And all kinds of looks went acrost his face. Sad, happy, worried, confused, you name it. When he finally found his tongue, it was to ask, "You mean he actually talked to you, Annie?"

It appeared no one believed me about that. "Yes, sir," I said. And then I told him the story of what happened, and he listened to every word. I had the feeling that *he* did believe me. And, you know, I could of swore I saw a tear in his eye before he turned around and blowed his nose.

"You're a brave little girl," he said at last. "And for what it's worth, I think you're right. If I ever saw lonely personified, it was in Be More Happy. You just keep on being yourself, and we'll see what happens. Okay?"

"Okay," I said. I didn't always understand Doc Elder when he talked. But I felt like I knowed what he meant anyhow. Before I left his store, I had promised to tell him the next time I talked to Be More.

On the way home Lou didn't talk much. She don't like it when someone else gets the attention. I didn't really care, though, 'cause I was thinking about going back over to Be More's house. Them boys was sure to be up to their tricks again, and Be More would be needing a friend.

Soon as lunch was over, I went on down to his house and was looking into them big sad eyes again. We sat out under that big tree, watching birds bathe in the dirt and talking about what a dry year it's been.

"Be okay," he said, "as long as the wells hold out. When the wells start going dry, you got trouble."

"Daddy says in a week or two, we'll be wishing it'd stop raining."

He looked at me with his big bushy white eyebrows raised. "Your daddy knows about things like that, for sure?"

I smiled 'cause I knowed nobody could say for sure about the weather, but folks roundabouts put a lot of stock in who come the closest to getting their predictions right.

"Reckon no one knows for sure," I said, "but Daddy's most always right." Then I said what I come to say. I told him about Billy and Jerry coming back and being anxious to play a trick on him, so he best be on the lookout.

That old look come back on his face, and he stared off into the woods in one direction, so I stared off in the other direction. I knowed he was lonely and was really nice, but no matter how hard I tried, that look still scared me. So I said, "Reckon I better be getting along." And looked up to see them big sad eyes on me.

"You got places to go, Annie, or do you just want to be rid of an old spook?"

He always knowed what I was thinking. But I didn't let on. I had to say something, and fast, so as not to hurt his feelings. That's when the idea first hit me. "I'm gonna go clear off a place to play ball. That place crost from the mailboxes don't have too many trees. Maybe there."

He didn't say nothing, just nodded.

I said, "See you, Be More." And when he didn't say nothing again, I looked back to see what was wrong, but he was staring off into the woods again, so I just left.

Boy, was it hot! I could smell the brush baking in the sun. It had that sweet smell that always made me hungry. If someone was to strike a match roundabouts, there'd surely be a forest fire. Reckon a little rain couldn't hurt nothing, for sure.

Back on the road, I watched the little clouds of dust that sprang up around my feet while I walked. There I was, alone again. Weren't nothing wrong with being alone. Especially if not being alone meant being with them boys.

It was like thinking of them made them appear, 'cause there they was sure as life. Mama always warned me that if I thought about bad things, they was sure to happen. "Think on good things and good will come to you," she said. I wish I'd paid more mind.

"Been visiting that crazy old man again?" Freddy Wayne asked real sickly sweet, and all the other boys started giggling like it was funny.

"He ain't crazy, Freddy Wayne. And I'll visit whoever I please!" I answered.

Billy and Jerry come out of the woods then, and by the look on their faces, Freddy Wayne had already told them everything he wanted them to know. Then, like he was scared I was gonna tell them my side, he said real quick, "Come on, Billy, Jerry. Like attracts like. She's probably as crazy as that old man." And that brought on more of that silly snickering and giggling.

Mostly, though, it was just Freddy Wayne, Jimmy, and Charles Edward. Bobby weren't laughing and neither was Billy or Jerry.

They all walked on off into the woods, and of course, I did a dumb thing. I kicked a rock with my bare foot. Hurt my own self when I really wanted to hurt them boys! I looked back to where they had walked away, and Bobby was still standing there. We just looked at each other, didn't say nothing, and finally, he turned around and poked on off.

Bobby was a puzzle. He hung around with them boys, but he didn't always go along with what Freddy Wayne said. He didn't disagree, but he didn't agree either. If I live to be two hundred years old, I won't never forget him pulling that rug out from under Freddy Wayne up to the clubhouse. I wonder if Freddy Wayne ever got after him for that.

If you are wondering what happened to Danny, why he ain't never with them boys anymore, it was like I said. When Mama and Daddy heard about that clubhouse, Danny was told that he better stay closer to home until he learnt not to play with matches or draw dirty pictures.

Anyhow, I got things to do. Course, I may be wasting my time clearing a softball field what with the way them boys feel about me. Wouldn't matter if I was Dizzy Dean, they wouldn't play ball with me now. Reckon

I'll find out soon enough. I stood there acrost from the mailboxes, looking at what was gonna be a ball field. Weren't too many trees, that was the good part, but there was a lot of brush and junk and a old log right in the middle of things, you might know.

I worked for a long time just clearing out rocks and boards and bottles. Then I decided I'd have to go home to get Daddy's big clippers and weed cutter before I could do much more. Walking backward, looking at what I had done, I tripped over that old log, but I didn't never hit the ground 'cause someone caught me. Be More Happy. Scared me silly!

"You walk frontwards, the way the good Lord intended, and you won't be getting scared by spooky old men," he said, and stood me back up on my feet.

I think he meant it to be funny. But I couldn't tell for sure. "Thanks, Be More," I said. I was embarrassed not only for falling but 'cause he had noticed how badly he had scared me.

"Looks like you could use a little help here," he said, and he brushed the hair back out of his face.

"Yeah," I said. "I was just gonna go get a weed cutter and things like that." Then I pointed to the pile of junk I had picked up. "That's what I done so far. Reckon there's more junk than I counted on."

We both stood looking at the pile of old bottles, cans, and rocks. "That only means it will take longer than I planned," I said.

"Might not take so long if you had help," Be More said.

"Probably not, but it ain't likely them boys is gonna want to help me."

"Why not? Boys that don't like softball? I never heard of such a thing!"

I think he knowed why not. He just wanted me to come out and say it. But I weren't gonna do it 'cause it was stupid. They didn't have no reason to be mean to Be More Happy. "Anyhow, me and Lou and Danny can play scrub," I said, and picked up a big rock to add to the heap.

Be More watched while I picked up a few more things and then said, "If you were to push that end and I this end, it wouldn't take a whole lot to move this old log."

He was wrong. Maybe if I had been a boy, I'd of been stronger. But they was days I just had to admit I was a girl. Bad as I hated it.

It was then something strange happened. We was pushing with everything we had, and not getting very far, when out of the woods walked Bobby. Without saying a word, he got down and started pushing, too.

We finally got that old log over to one side, out of the way. While we was all admiring our work, Bobby asked, "What you clearing for, Annie?" He was very careful not to even look at Be More.

"Thought we could use a place to play ball," I said. "Reckon it turned out to be more work than I planned on, though."

"Yeah, I guess so," he said and wiped the sweat off his face.

Then we all started picking up junk, and before I knowed it, Bobby was gone. I reckoned it was more work than he counted on, too.

Now let me tell you, I seen things that has surprised me before, and I seen things that downright shocked me, but I ain't never seen nothing like what happened next. I had my head down trying to pry a big rock out of the ground with a stick when I heard this swishing sound. I recognized right off what the sound was, but I couldn't figure it out, unless Be More had gone home and come back with a weed cutter. But it weren't Be More. There he stood right in front of me, and from the look on his face, he was as surprised as I was about to be.

That swishing sound was coming from Freddy Wayne and Jimmy. They was working up a big sweat cutting weeds down. Charles Edward and Bobby was up in that big oak with a saw, getting ready to cut off a branch that hung out over the field, and Billy and Jerry was picking out rocks faster than me and Be More ever done.

Nobody said nothing for a long time. I was uncomfortable 'cause I didn't know what Be More thought. But it all worked out good. After a while, them boys started talking and making jokes like they always do, and the look on Be More's face was almost happy. It weren't long before we had a regular softball field.

When all the work was done, it was awkward. Them boys didn't know what to say, and it was for sure Be More weren't about to say nothing. Finally, I said, "Thanks, boys. I reckon it was a lot more of a job than I thought it was gonna be."

"Weren't too much for all of us, though," Bobby said.

Billy and Jerry, sensing the tension in the air, decided it was suppertime and left, saying they'd be back tomorrow.

"Make it around ten and bring your ball and glove!" Charles Edward hollered to them after they had left.

Freddy Wayne kicked a rock around on the ground and then took to shining his glasses. He was embarrassed that he didn't know what to say. That didn't surprise me, though. He never could think of nothing good to say and, right then, there weren't nothing bad to be said.

Next thing I knowed, all them boys had disappeared. I turned around and looked at Be More. I like to read what's on people's faces, but I couldn't read his just then. It was sad and happy at the same time.

"They ain't bad once you get to know them, huh, Be More?" I said.

He looked off into the woods after them for a while, then he said. "Just boys, Annie. Just boys."

Chapter 7

You should of seen the look on Mama's face when I got home. I reckon I was kind of dirty, but dirty ain't bad. It was worth it. I slept like a log that night, and believe it or not, when I got up the next morning, Lou and Danny was already sitting at the breakfast table. It weren't that I was late neither. They was that excited about playing ball.

Danny was fussing about having to eat his egg. If it was up to him, all he'd ever eat would be biscuits and jelly, but when it come to hardheads, I guess Mama had everyone beat. And eggs was one thing she was set on. There was other things, too, like squash, and liver, and fish, but eggs was our main pain. Not that we didn't like eggs, but they weren't always time to sit down and be nice about eating. A biscuit and jelly you could grab and run with. Anyhow, Danny didn't have no better sense than to argue with Mama. Guess he hadn't been around long enough to learn better.

Finally, when we was all nicely fed, we ran on over to the ball field. The only equipment we could find was Danny's old red ball cap. I was sure hoping everyone else had better luck, but the sad bunch of boys I seen waiting at the ball field told that they didn't.

"You ain't got no ball?" Freddy Wayne hollered at me, like I ought to have a whole bag full of balls, bats, gloves, and stuff.

I was dumfounded and just shook my head while Junior answered back, "You ain't got no ball either, Freddy Wayne. Don't go yelling at Annie. Nobody yelled at you." And then to me and Lou he said, "Ain't none of us got nothing."

I looked around at all the sad faces. I should of guessed it. All the ball fields in the world wasn't gonna help us. As it happened, the only ball that showed up was Jimmy's, and it was the most chewed up thing I ever saw. Bobby's bat was cracked right up the middle, and Junior's was warped from lying outside most of last winter.

We all sat around kicking up dirt and chucking rocks out into the woods. I reckon we was waiting for a bolt of lightning to strike and produce a whole clutch of balls and bats.

Well, that's nearly what did happen. We'd been sitting around for almost a hour when Be More Happy come walking out of the woods. He looked surprised to see us all there, but I don't think it was for real. I think he knowed exactly what was going on.

Nobody said good morning or nothing. Be More come on over to where I was sitting on a stump.

"Morning, Be More," I said.

"Good morning, Annie." Then he looked around at all them that was trying so hard to pretend he weren't there. "Why all the sad faces?" he asked. And then, looking at that pitiful old chewed-up ball on the ground, he said, "No ball, huh?" That was just like Be More. He always knowed what was going on without ever having to be told.

"No ball, no bat, no nothing," I said. "Just one really nice place to play ball." I laughed, and Be More just nodded.

We stood around for a while longer. I could see Be More was thinking on something. I could also see the sideways looks them boys was giving him. It was just Freddy Wayne, Jimmy, Charles Edward, and Billy that was looking mean. Junior and Bobby was sitting on that old log listening to Lou tell them all about singing with Johnny Brown last Sunday. I wonder if she'll ever get tired of talking about that. Anyhow, Danny and Jerry was off to one side snapping beetles. So the only ones to worry on was them mean ones. I say mean, but they was all good enough when they wasn't around Freddy Wayne. He has a mean streak in him that could sour milk!

I got cold chills down my back when Freddy Wayne throwed down his ball real hard and started walking on off. He was headed right for me and Be More.

I heard Be More draw in his breath like he was gonna say something, and I thought for a minute he was gonna talk to Freddy Wayne. But no, he says to me kind of loud, "I suppose he has to go to work?" He raised one eyebrow at me, but I didn't know what he meant.

I said, "Freddy Wayne don't work, Be More, he's just going home to pout."

Freddy Wayne had froze in his tracks when he heard what Be More said. And looking at him standing there, it come across to me, too. Nobody else seemed to know what was going on. Then Freddy Wayne turned around like that bolt of lightning we was all waiting for finally struck.

"I got it!" he yelped. "I got it!"

Junior was getting curious at what all was going on, and come over to where Freddy Wayne was. "What you got, Freddy Wayne?" he asked. And all the other kids started edging up.

"We can all work at doing odd jobs around, and earn enough money to buy some new bats and balls!" He was excited and had his glasses off, polishing them up a mile a minute.

Junior's face looked like somebody just turned on a light. And everybody else was hitting Freddy Wayne around like he was some kind of a hero. But I knowed who the hero was. The hero was the old man who nodded and gave me a big wink right before he walked on off into the woods.

"Freddy Wayne," Junior said, "that's the best idea you ever had." He looked at all the rest of us and said, "Hey gang, what do you say? Looks like Freddy Wayne done had a idea. You want to try it?"

Everyone agreed so loud you would of thought there was forty kids instead of just ten out in them woods.

It weren't easy, but Junior got things quieted down, and somehow took over what Freddy Wayne would of been doing. Freddy Wayne weren't taking it too kindly, but he weren't about to say nothing, what with his lip just getting well from the last time he crossed Junior. It did me good to see Freddy Wayne getting whittled down to size.

Billy and Jerry was the first to settle on what they was gonna do. "Granny will let us use the lawnmower," Billy said, "and I bet we can earn five, maybe six dollars between now and Monday."

Freddy Wayne snickered real loud, and Junior looked at him hard, and said to Billy, "Sounds good, Bill. You just do your best."

"I can paint real good," Danny squealed, bouncing up and down in front of Junior.

"We'll see. We'll see. Just hang on to yourself," Junior said, turning him around and swatting him over to where me and Lou was sitting on the ground. The look on poor Junior's face was begging for help.

Freddy Wayne and Jimmy had their heads together whispering something. I hoped it weren't trouble they was planning, and it weren't.

"Peanuts!" Jimmy sputtered. "We can sell peanuts. Freddy Wayne says we can, and we can." Jimmy's face was always red, and his nose was runny. His nose was always runny. I reckon he was a good enough person if it weren't for living with Freddy Wayne.

Junior spoke up again. "Is that right, Freddy Wayne? You think you could get the job?"

The *job* was selling peanuts at Travelers' Field. There was a game that night, so all they had to do was ask Mr. Lasiter. From what I hear, Mr. Lasiter is a good friend, so it shouldn't be too hard.

"Sure we can," Freddy Wayne said with a scowl. "Mr. Lasiter said anytime we needed the money, the job was ours."

"Great!" Junior said, and turned to me and Lou. "What do you think you girls can do?"

We looked at each other for a while, and finally, Lou said, like it was dirty or something, "I guess we could wash windows." Lou never took kindly to working. She always had better things to do.

"Wash windows?" Junior asked, looking at me for agreement. I reckon he knowed I'd be doing most of the washing.

"Wash windows," I said with a grimace, and Danny laughed. He knew how much I hated to wash windows, and that delighted him.

While me and Lou was making our plans, Danny snuck away from us and run up to Junior, tugging on his shirttail. "I can build things, too. Daddy showed me how. I can really build things."

Junior laughed. "Okay, Danny boy, we'll think on it. Give me a minute, hear?"

Charles Edward spoke up then. "Me and Bobby is gonna wash cars up at Hillcrest, okay?" Bobby nodded the whole time Charles Edward was talking.

Junior squinted his eyes up like he was thinking real hard on something. Then he started nodding. "That's good, Charles Edward, Bobby. I could help out too. Where did you have in mind, the Gulf Station?"

"Yeah," Bobby said. "My daddy knows Mr. Blanchard. He can set it up. I'm sure he can." Bobby was always at his best when he was being helpful. No matter how much he hung around with them boys, he couldn't never be quite as mean.

"Then it's settled," Junior announced. "Let's all get to work and meet back here first thing Monday morning to count up our money and see what we can get."

Everyone started to leave, but a loud, "Hrrumff!" stopped us all cold. Can you believe it? It was Danny! I never heard such a loud and really serious noise come from that boy before.

"You forgot about me, Junior," he said, kind of indignant-like. "I can do lots of things."

Junior was clearly embarrassed. Forgetting Danny was the kind of thing Freddy Wayne would do, and Freddy Wayne weren't no one he would want to be like. He hushed all the snickering from the older boys, and putting his arm across Danny's shoulder, he led him over to an old stump and sat down.

"Now let's see," he said. "What do y'all reckon old Danny can do?"

Freddy Wayne tittered but got real quiet when he seen the look on Junior's face.

Junior snapped his fingers and jumped up. "I got it, how about pop bottles? You can collect pop bottles and turn them in up to Mrs. Bybee's store for money."

Danny was happy with his assignment, but not too terribly thrilled. I could tell he'd rather be painting or building a house for someone, but bottles it would have to be.

We all started off to do our jobs. When we come to the other side of the woods, we could hear Freddy Wayne's voice. He was laughing and saying something about pop bottles. Danny didn't say nothing, but his face sure turned red. Near as red as his hair. What I wouldn't give to put my foot in Freddy Wayne's big mouth. I told Danny that if the truth was known, I'd rather be looking for bottles than washing windows.

When we got back home, Lou told me that she didn't want to work that afternoon. She suggested that I go out and get the jobs and we could do them Saturday. So that's what I did. I most always ended up doing whatever Lou told me to do.

I was off, going from door to door. Sounds bad, but they ain't more than nine houses in the whole neighborhood. Danny had disappeared, and I didn't reckon I'd be seeing hide nor hair of him until he done what he thought was a good job. Anyhow, I picked up all the bottles I seen along the way. I figured he'd be needing a little help. By suppertime, I had sore feet and only two jobs lined up. Granny said she'd pay ten cents if we'd wash her kitchen windows. And Doc Elder was gonna give us fifty cents to wash his front window. That didn't seem like a whole lot of money to me. I found six bottles along "H" Street on the way down to Doc Elder's place, and I reckoned how maybe we all ought to be out hunting bottles instead of washing windows.

While I was peeling potatoes for supper, I told Mama about our two little jobs, and I reckon she felt sorry for us. She said if we would wash the windows in the front room, she'd give a quarter. That was eighty-five cents. Not too bad.

Like I said, I most didn't see Danny over the weekend. He come in just in time for supper, and most times, fell asleep right after. I asked him once how it was going, and all he would say was that he was gonna make more money than any of them. I admired his spunk, but I felt sorry for him at the same time.

That Saturday, Lou really surprised me. She worked ever' bit as hard as I did. At the end of the day, we had shriveled hands, tired backs, and eighty-five cents to show for our work.

Come Monday morning, I was almost embarrassed to go up to the ball field with just eighty-five cents. I could hear Freddy Wayne snickering before we ever left the house. Danny was up and out before me and Lou even got out of bed. That boy acts so strange sometimes, but I reckon he was feeling bad same as I was.

When we got to the ball field, everybody was there ahead of us again. Everybody but Danny. Freddy Wayne was strutting around like a banty rooster. Him and Jimmy had brought in the four dollars they earned selling peanuts at the ball game.

Billy and Jerry was almost as disgusted as me and Lou. They mowed grass until dark on Friday, and all day long Saturday and only got one dollar.

Charles Edward, Junior, and Bobby was pretty proud of the dollar and fifty cents they made washing cars. And Junior told the funniest thing on Old Man Fox.

Old Man Fox is a dirty person. Seems like ever place he goes, flies just foller him around. He drives a black truck, sort of like Be More's, only it is so dirty it's hard to believe. The bad thing is, he chews tobacco, and when he chews, he spits. Don't make no matter where he is, he just spits. So anyhow, the whole side of his truck is plain covered with spit out chewing tobacco. Yuck! Them three boys seen him up to Hillcrest Saturday afternoon and seen their chance to make a lot of money. But as it happened, the old man was downright insulted. Said his truck weren't dirty. He drove off in a huff, leaving behind a whole swarm of unhappy flies.

Junior counted up the money. There was seven dollars and thirty-five cents. We weren't too happy, but we reckoned it would have to do. We was all heading out to walk up to Hillcrest, when Danny come running through the woods.

"Wait!" he hollered. "Wait for me, you ain't got my money yet." His face was red like he run a mile or two.

Freddy Wayne snickered and called out ahead, "Hey Junior, pipsqueak here wants to put in his two cents' worth!" Then he spit on the ground right at Danny's feet. I pulled Danny away, giving Freddy Wayne the ugliest look I had to give.

"Sorry, Danny boy," Junior said. "Didn't reckon you was coming." Then he ruffed up Danny's hair and said, "Let's have it, money pockets."

You never seen faces like I seen when Danny started pulling money out of his pockets. By the time he was finished, he pulled out five dollars and nine cents. Freddy Wayne was speechless, of course, 'cause they weren't nothing bad to say.

I was proud of Danny that day, but not half so proud as he was of hisself. On the way up to Hillcrest, them boys all took turns carrying him on their shoulders, even Freddy Wayne. He didn't like it, but he done it 'cause Junior said to. And I swear, for all his wiggling around, Danny seemed to enjoy the ride on Freddy Wayne's shoulders more than any of the others.

Chapter 8

We didn't do much else for the rest of that week but play ball. Some days we'd even carry a sandwich and a jar of iced tea to the ball field so as we wouldn't even have to go home for lunch.

Danny played, too. He weren't much good. I reckon that's 'cause he was so little. Somehow or the other, he always managed to get hisself on Freddy Wayne's team. That didn't make Freddy Wayne too happy. He wanted all the good guys on his team, 'cause it was real important to him to win. I could of told Freddy Wayne it weren't smart to make Danny mad, but he probably wouldn't of listened anyway. Now he'll just have to put up with the little redheaded devil till things cool off.

I mean to tell you, them days was hot! I couldn't even recollect when it last rained. Everyday all the gardens had to be watered, and I was worried to death over that watermelon. Be More said it would be okay, and I reckon he knowed what he was talking about.

Twice that week, Daddy had to get up in the middle of the night and go help fight forest fires. They scared me. Sometimes I could see the orange blazes up on the hill right from my own window. But they was far enough away they didn't do no damage, except to the woods, and that was sad. Real sad.

Friday morning we was all so happy. Around eleven o'clock, the wind come up, and clouds started rolling in. Mean-looking clouds. I was glad, but my stomach didn't know it. It kept turning over like it always does when it storms.

The rain come. A real gully washer! I thought it was nice, but Daddy and Mama said it wouldn't do no good. Said what we needed was a long slow rain. Grownups ain't always easy to please. They want things just one way, and nothing else will do.

Around two o'clock, the rain quit. They was still clouds in the sky, but the thunder and lightning was gone. So I reckoned it was over for the most part and went on out to see what all was going on. Weren't much. No one was around. Lou wouldn't come out. She didn't want to get her feet muddy. Danny come out with me, but he stopped at the first mud puddle he seen, and he stayed.

I walked on over to Aunt Dorothy's. Junior and Charles Edward was playing checkers on the front porch. You should of seen the creek by their house. The water was clean over the top of the bridge.

"Annie, don't you get too close there, you'll get pulled right in," Junior hollered at me from his porch.

I shuddered just thinking about it and come on back away. Then I started to wondering about Be More. I knowed his house was up off the ground, but … but you can't never tell, and that place down there floods all the time. So I headed on down to his place, squishing the mud between my toes as I walked along. It felt good. The whole place smelled good, too. I love to smell the woods right after it rains. Smells clean.

Old Man Fox passed me in his ugly old truck. He didn't wave or nothing. I looked back at the tracks in the road to see where he had come from, and sure enough, he come right over that bridge that was covered over with water. That crazy old man!

I follered the road on down toward Be More's. When I come close to his place, I could see old Man Fox's truck stopped in the middle of the road right before he come to the creek. I wondered if maybe that bridge had washed out. There sure was a lot of water.

Then I noticed Old Man Fox weren't the only one there. Mr. Weaver was there. He was standing close to the water waving his walking stick at something. And I seen Freddy Wayne standing on the far side of the creek, close to Doc Elder, his pants legs was rolled up like he was planning on walking across that bridge. If there was still a bridge to cross. Then I seen something terrible! Right there in all that ugly, muddy water, a white head come bobbing up. Be More! My stomach took a turn like it never done before, and my legs like to give out on me. What was Be More doing in that water? He was drowning for sure. I knew it.

When I started to run on down there, a car come up behind me. It was Mama and Daddy. Almost before the car stopped, Mama was out of it. She grabbed me up and was hugging and kissing and crying all to once. I couldn't make heads nor tails out of what she was saying. Something about Mrs. Bybee and some kids. Then she stopped dead, and started shaking me and yelling, "Where's Danny, Annie? Where's Danny?"

Daddy had got out of the car and come around by then. He tried to make Mama be still and she finally was when I said, "Danny's up to the ball field playing in the mud." I turned to Daddy and asked, "What's wrong?" Then it was I remembered Be More in the creek. I yelled out, "Be More!" and started to run again, but Daddy grabbed hold of me and pushed me into the car. Just as we stopped behind Old Man Fox's truck, another car coming fast pulled up behind us.

Aunt Dorothy jumped out of her car. She weren't smiling and her face was near as white as Mama's. "Good Lord!" she said under her breath. "Did they find them?" At least she knowed where her boys was 'cause they was just coming out of the back seat of her car.

Everybody took off for the edge of the creek where Mr. Weaver was. Seemed like all of them but me knowed what was going on. I started to foller them, and I heard this terrible wailing sound. It was Freddy Wayne. Crying! Doc Elder had his arm around him trying to give comfort, but Freddy Wayne just kept right on crying.

Down at the edge of the creek, I seen Be More come up out of the water. He handed a half drowned boy out of the water to Daddy, and then slid back in. It was Bobby! He was kicking and spewing and making a terrible fuss. It weren't no time till Be More come crawling out of the water dragging Jimmy along with him. Mama and Daddy and Aunt Dorothy grabbed on to them boys and started fussing over them like they was their own. Daddy got the blanket out of the back of the car and wrapped them up in it, then shoved them into the back seat.

No one paid any attention to Be More. He was sitting on a rock over by the edge of the creek, coughing, and shaking the water out of his long white hair. Finally, as Daddy and Aunt Dorothy drove off, Doc Elder put Freddy Wayne in his car and very carefully come on across the bridge. He got out and went straight to Be More, shrugged off his coat and laid it across Be More's shoulders.

Mr. Weaver and Old Man Fox was trying to get Freddy Wayne to go on home, but he weren't gonna have it. He sure was acting strange. That was his brother just dragged out of the creek, and he wouldn't even pay him no mind. Nothing Freddy Wayne did was what you'd call normal. Finally, they gave up and made Junior and Charles Edward promise to see him on home. Junior agreed to do it, but he never looked directly at Freddy Wayne's face 'cause it was still all red from crying.

Then it was something happened what made my blood run cold. I heard a siren coming from the direction of town. The sheriff. Be More jumped like he was shot and headed off toward the woods, but our eyes caught each other, and he stopped cold. He looked like he wanted to say something but couldn't. Then he run on off into the woods. Main thing that bothered me was the look in his eyes. It was just like that first time. So alone. So empty. But even with all that, I could tell that he was scared, too.

Problem was, I weren't the only one seen it. When I turned around, I seen all of them was looking. Doc Elder and Mr. Weaver was looking after him like they was as worried as I was. I don't reckon I can rightly tell you what all I seen on Freddy Wayne's face. There was hate there, and a kind of a look that says, "Now I got you!" Like he would look at a rabbit he caught in a trap.

Then it was Doc Elder who took control of things. He didn't ask nobody nothing. He took hold of Freddy Wayne by the elbow, walked him around and shoved him into Old Man Fox's truck.

"Mr. Fox," he said, "it appears to me that this young man needs a ride home. If you don't mind?"

Old Man Fox spit on the ground, looked into the woods where Be More run off, and said with a big grin, "Don't mind a little bit." Then he jumped in his truck, started up, and left before Freddy Wayne had time to say whatever was on his mind.

Me and Junior and Charles Edward was standing there watching the whole thing with our mouths hanging open. When the sheriff's car could be seen coming down Hayes Street, Doc Elder turned to us and said, "Junior, I'm trusting you and Charles Edward to see Annie on home." When we didn't move, he said, "Now!" There weren't no arguing with the tone of voice he used.

We walked on off, back up the hill. I reckon we was all just about as confused as we'd ever be. About halfway up the hill, we turned around and looked back. The sheriff's car was there on this side of the creek. Doc Elder and Mr. Weaver was talking to him. Then Doc Elder put his arm across the sheriff's shoulders, and they walked over to his car. I'd of give anything to hear what Doc Elder was saying. Whatever it was, it seemed to set all right with the sheriff, 'cause he got in his car and drove off. Mr. Weaver and Doc Elder talked for a minute, then Doc Elder got in his car and left, and Mr. Weaver stared into the creek a while before he walked on off.

Junior said, "What do you make of that?" more to himself than to me or Charles Edward. Then we heard someone running up behind us, and turned around to see a mud covered Danny coming up fast.

"What's the siren?" he puffed. "Is it a fire?"

"A fire on a day like this?" Junior teased. "That'd be a sight," and Charles Edward laughed. First sound I heard him make since this all started.

I dragged Danny on home and told him about Jimmy and Bobby along the way. I didn't say nothing about the rest. That was gonna take some thinking on. I didn't go in when we got back to the house. Mama wasn't gonna be happy about all that mud on Danny, but maybe she wouldn't be too mad. The way she was acting a little while ago, she'd be glad if I brung him home coated in dog doodoo.

Instead of going in, I went on over to Freddy Wayne and Jimmy's house to see how Jimmy was. Bobby was there, too. Aunt Virginia had insisted on him staying there, 'cause Bobby's mother was sick, and she didn't think it would be good to excite her.

I have to tell you, Aunt Virginia weren't really my aunt. That's just what everybody called her. She was a nice enough lady, and I'd be proud if she was my aunt, but she weren't. I never could understand how she could be Freddy Wayne's mother, either. I always thought it was more likely that Freddy Wayne just crawled out from under a rock.

Junior and Charles Edward was over there, too. They all was talking about what happened. I say all, but that weren't actually true. Junior and Charles Edward was asking plenty of questions, but whenever anyone started to answer, Freddy Wayne would interrupt and drown them out. He was awful nervous about something. Whenever Aunt Virginia would leave the room, Freddy Wayne would start ranting about Be More, like he had been the cause of everything that happened down at the creek.

The only thing I found out, and I found that out from Junior, was that Mrs. Bybee had seen the boys go into the water from her store up on Hayes Street. She was the one called everybody. Bobby kept trying to say something but couldn't get a word in for Freddy Wayne. Finally I had enough of his bullying and went on home.

Later that night, after supper, Daddy had to go down to Doc Elder's to get a magazine to read, so I went along. While Daddy was looking at the magazines, I talked to Doc Elder. It weren't easy at first, 'cause I sensed he didn't want to talk.

"What did the sheriff say, Doc?" I started.

He looked over to where Daddy was reading, and then put down the glass he was polishing. "Annie, I know you must be very curious about what happened down there." He looked back over at Daddy. "Can you trust me, sweet Annie? What I did, I did for Be More. I'm sure you would have done the same thing. The way things are going with you and Be More, you'll probably know all you want to soon enough, but for now, you'll have to trust me."

Daddy had found his magazine and come over to where we was. Looked like I didn't have any choice. I weren't gonna get no more than that out of Doc Elder. At least not right then.

On the way home Daddy asked, "What were you and Doc Elder whispering about?"

"We was just talking about Be More Happy, and what happened this afternoon," I said, and wondered if only half of the truth was the same thing as a lie.

"He sure did a good thing. Lucky he was there," Daddy said, shaking his head from side to side. "Not many men would of jumped into that creek the way he did. Of course, they ain't many people alive so dumb as to try to cross a bridge that's clean covered up with water, either." He drove on for a while, and then said, "Wonder whatever prompted them to do that? Freddy Wayne didn't cross. Looks like he could of warned them other two off."

I wondered too. There was a lot to wonder about that night; Doc Elder, and what he told the sheriff; Be More, and the way he acted when he heard that siren; them crazy boys that should of had better sense than to do what they done; and Freddy Wayne. Freddy Wayne was always something to wonder on.

In bed that night, I had a hard time getting to sleep. I reckon Lou was busy wondering on things, too, 'cause she weren't talking like she usually does. Maybe that was why I had trouble getting to sleep. Anyhow, when I woke up in the middle of the night, I wished I hadn't gone to sleep at all.

I dreamed about Be More running through the woods with the sheriff after him. He was all ragged and tired. Then he weren't being chased no more. He was down at the creek, and while Doc Elder and Mr. Weaver sat and watched, Be More was drowning all them boys, one at a time, and laughing like the devil the whole while he was doing it.

Chapter 9

The next morning didn't start off too good. I woke up with a freckle-faced boy staring down at me from where he was sitting on my stomach.

"Wake up, you lazy thing," Danny said, and then started bouncing up and down, chanting, "Lazy bones, lazy bones, Annie is a lazy bones."

I rolled over, taking him with me, grabbed a pillow, and stuffed it in his face. While he was squirming around trying to get loose, I seen he was right, I was lazy! Lou was already up, and it looked to be late in the morning.

I lifted the pillow off the squirming creature that was underneath me. "Don't you know how to wake a person up?" I screeched. "You can ruin a whole day like that, you little varmint. Now get out of here before I call Mama."

Danny got off the bed, walked over to the vanity, and started combing on his hair. "Just thought you might want to know ..." Then I seen the devil light up in his face. He weren't about to give nothing away.

"Know what?" I asked, and I seen he weren't gonna tell, so I throwed the pillow at him. It never got there, though. Mama caught it when she walked in. I could tell that was gonna be a bad day.

"Danny, there's trash waiting to be burned," she said as she threw my pillow back to me. He left with a grin on his face 'cause he was getting by without telling me whatever it was he was itching to say.

Saturday mornings was my favorite. We always had pancakes. Mama didn't have to argue any of us into eating our pancakes. While I was eating, Lou was in the front room practicing her piano lesson. Then Danny come back in and sat grinning at me while I ate. I reckoned if he was that anxious to keep something from me, it wouldn't be any time till he let it out. So I decided to ignore him.

"We going to the store today, Mama?" I asked.

"Soon as Daddy gets home," she said.

For some reason, that upset Danny. He got up and run over to Mama. "When's that? When's he gonna be home?"

"Sometime around noon," she answered, and studied Danny real hard. "You sure are acting strange this morning. Could it have anything to do with them boys coming here?"

"No!" he said, a bit too quick. Then he quit fooling around and told it. "Freddy Wayne called a special meeting up to the clubhouse and said for all three of us to come."

"Girls at the clubhouse," Mama said. "Isn't that a little unusual?"

Danny just shrugged.

I was busy remembering the last time I went up there. I weren't about to go through all that again. But I knowed if Lou was there, they'd be just as sweet as sugar. So I decided if she was gonna go, I'd go.

She went. I was glad, 'cause I had a idea what it was all about, and I wanted to be there when Freddy Wayne started telling his tales.

They was all waiting when we got there. Freddy Wayne seemed to be in charge, but it made me feel good to see Junior standing over in the corner, chewing on a straw.

Freddy Wayne looked at me and sneered. He wouldn't say what he wanted to, 'cause of Junior, and he weren't about to make a fool of hisself in front of Lou.

"This here meeting is called to order," he said at last. Then he took off his glasses and started polishing them up. "I reckon some of you already know what this is all about." He looked at everybody. "That old man, Be More Happy."

Then he went on and told about what happened when Be More heard the siren, and how Doc Elder run everybody off. He had everybody's attention all right. There weren't a sound to be heard in the place except for Jimmy's constant, drawn-out sniffles.

Lou looked at me and mouthed, "Is this true?" and I nodded.

Freddy Wayne seen that, grinned real mean-like, and decided to rub it in a little. "I want those of you who saw what happened, to tell if I ain't telling the truth."

Nobody said nothing.

"Let's hear it," he said. "Ain't it the truth, Junior?"

Junior nodded.

"Charles Edward?"

"It's true," Charles Edward said, like the words tasted bad in his mouth.

"Annie?"

I just looked at him hard. I weren't about to answer, and he knowed it.

He cleared his throat real official-like and said, "Well, fellow club members," and nodding to me and Lou, added, "and visitors, I think it's time we was finding out something about that old man. You see what happened the minute we let down our guard. Them strange things started happening again."

I couldn't swear to it, but it sounded to me like he was hinting that Be More was the cause of them boys falling in the creek.

Next, he looks right square at me and says, "Some of us here ain't too careful about the friends we make. Ain't no telling about a person what runs at the sound of a sheriff's siren. Could be he's done murdered some what weren't smart enough to know him for what he is. Could be he's from some foreign country, or worse than that, he could even be from some other planet for all we know." He paused there to make sure he was scaring everyone proper. The only ones what looked worried was Jimmy, Charles Edward, Billy, Jerry and worst of all, Danny. His eyes was round as saucers.

Junior had a half-smile on his face. He knowed better. And Lou looked like she just plain didn't care, as long as she could hurry up and get out of that place.

Bobby was different. He had something on his mind for sure, and he weren't at all scared by what Freddy Wayne said. It was like he weren't even scared of Freddy Wayne no more.

I think Freddy Wayne seen that he was losing some of us, so he hurried on. "What we are gonna do is have an investigation. I want everybody here to find something out about that old man and be back here right after lunch on Monday to tell it." He looked at me and seen he hadn't put the proper scare into me, and said, "Whoever don't bring back some kind of news on him will have to answer to all the members of this here club." He stared at me till I turned around and left out of there.

"Annie, I don't think it's smart for you to be the way you are with Freddy Wayne," Lou said while we was walking back home.

"I don't care if it's smart or not," I said. "He's ugly, and I can't stand the way he acts."

We was quiet for a spell. You'd of thought they'd been talking hex up there by the look of Danny. Finally, when he spoke up, his voice was shaking. "You're gonna do it, ain't you, Annie? You're gonna find something out, ain't you?"

I didn't answer for a long time. Then I said, "Don't make no matter. Freddy Wayne will be mad anyway, 'cause whatever I find out will be something nice."

We got home in time to go up to Hillcrest with Mama and Daddy. That was one of my favorite things to do. Daddy always give us a quarter, and we could go over to the variety store and spend it on anything we wanted, or sometimes we would go over to the bakery. It was hard to decide. We seen there was a Ma and Pa Kettle movie on at the Prospect, and Daddy promised we could see it that night.

I thought it over most of the afternoon, and before we left to go to the picture show, I told Lou and Danny that I was gonna see what I could find out about Be More. I told them they didn't have to do nothing, that I'd give them something to tell for Monday. Danny didn't care much for the idea, but after a few meaningful threats, he come around. Lou seemed relieved.

So it was, that first thing after church on Sunday, I was out looking for Mr. Weaver. I had waited too long to talk to Doc Elder. His store was closed on Sunday, and nobody ever bothered him Sundays unless it was an emergency. I just hoped Mr. Weaver was somewhere close by.

He was. I found him sitting by the creek up above Granny's house. I knowed he'd be there, 'cause I heard Rex barking, and anywhere you seen Rex, Mr. Weaver weren't far away.

He was wearing his white Sunday shirt, and was sitting on a big rock cooling his feet in the creek. I reckon he had been to church, too.

"Heidy, girl," he said, without even turning around.

"Heidy, Mr. Weaver," I said. "How'd you know it was me?"

"Dogs is smart when it comes to people. You're one of the few people roundabouts that old Rex there don't bark his head off at." He took a handkerchief out of his pocket and wiped his face.

"Oh," I said, and we sat for a while being quiet.

"Mr. Weaver," I said real soft, 'cause I wasn't sure if he was asleep or awake.

"What you need, girl?" he answered.

"Mr. Weaver," I started again, "can you tell me something about Be More Happy?"

He waited a long time before he answered, and then he said, "What you need to know for?"

"It's them boys," I said. "Ever since what happened the other day down by the creek, they been saying bad things about him again."

He waited for an awful long time before he answered back. I never could tell if he had gone to sleep or was just thinking. Sometimes I'd be talking away, and then find out he was sound asleep. That always made me feel so dumb. Finally he said, "Be More Happy ain't bad. Just unlucky. It weren't like it was his fault. Though they was those what said it was. Mostly the papers." He stopped there, as if to remember, and then went on, "Girl, don't you never believe what you read in them papers. They is all communists, you know." What he was saying didn't make no sense at all.

"It was their country-house then. Belonged to his daddy, and so did the truck. He's the one what painted Be More Happy crost the back, his daddy was. They was all so happy in them days. Then all that mess! All them ding-blasted busybodies! He just disappeared. Gone for years." Mr. Weaver stopped there, and I thought it was gonna be years before he started up talking again.

"Nobody knowed him when he come back. Didn't never talk to no one. Nothing." He started putting on his shoes and socks, so I reckoned it was about time to go.

"Thanks, Mr. Weaver," I said. "I knowed Be More weren't bad. I reckon I'll head on down by his house now, and make sure he's okay."

He looked straight at me for a while then he said, "Maybe you remind him of *her*, girl. You're the only one he talks to. Only one."

I couldn't make heads nor tails out of what he was saying, so I said, "See you, Mr. Weaver."

"See you, girl."

I left to go on down to Be More's. I didn't know what, but I'd find something good out of all the things he said and tell it on Monday.

"Annie!" Be More called when he seen me coming.

While I was walking on into his place, I thought how strange it was that when he weren't around, I was scared silly of him, but when he was close by, I knowed they weren't nothing to be scared of.

"How you doing, Be More?" I asked as I walked up.

"Fair. Fair. And you?" he said.

"I'm okay." I picked up a pan and helped him to feed his chickens.

"Who's your friend?" Be More asked, and I looked around to see Rex had follered me. That was strange, 'cause he didn't hardly ever leave Mr. Weaver. Something else strange was he weren't barking.

"That's Rex, Be More. He's Mr. Weaver's dog." I called him over to me, and he walked over real slow wagging his tail. Then he flopped down in the dirt right between me and Be More. When we went over to sit on the bench under that big tree, he follered us.

Be More didn't say nothing about what happened Friday.

We just talked chickens and watermelon, and then I took Rex on over to Mr. Weaver's house.

Mr. Weaver was out on his front porch. "Heidy, girl," he said as I come up. Rex run on up on the porch and lay down next to Mr. Weaver. The old man reached down and patted his head. "Old Rex been telling any secrets?"

We looked at each other long and hard, and then I knowed why Rex had follered me. Mr. Weaver sent him to tell me something, and he told me all right. Told me all I needed to know for Monday.

Monday finally come, but it seemed like a year between breakfast and lunch. Right after we ate, we went on up to the clubhouse. Jimmy and Bobby was outside and it looked to me like they been fussing about something. Jimmy's face was a whole lot redder than usual, and Bobby was awful quiet, like he had something on his mind.

Freddy Wayne called the meeting to order. Everybody was there but Junior, and when Billy asked about him, Freddy Wayne said, Junior had a guitar lesson or something." His face was red, too, and I wondered why he acted so nervous. "Let's get on with this. Ah, Billy, what did you find out?"

Billy stood up and twisted his hands while he said, "Not much. All Granny knowed was that he been around here near twenty years." He sat down, and Jerry patted him on the back.

Freddy Wayne looked disgusted. "Jerry, I hope you found out more!" he threatened.

Jerry kind of cowered behind Billy and said, "Granny was all we knowed to ask, and she didn't know nothing but what Billy said." Freddy Wayne was such a bully! I felt sorry for poor little Jerry.

I think he seen I was getting mad so he looked right at me and asked Lou what she found out.

"Annie's gonna tell what we learned," she answered.

Then I told them about Rex not barking at Be More, and reminded them how often old Rex had cornered all of them till he got tired out of fooling with them.

Freddy Wayne laughed like to make fun of me. "You mean to say that the old man is good 'cause a stupid old dog don't bark at him?" He banged his hands on the table and laughed some more. "You know what I think? I think you are purt near as dumb as that old dog. I think—"

He didn't get to say what else he was thinking, 'cause Bobby interrupted. "I think it's about time you was telling the truth, Freddy Wayne."

Freddy Wayne glared at him, and you could of heard a pin drop in that place.

Bobby's face was white and his voice shook as he went on. "The reason you was making such a big thing out of Be More Happy was 'cause you was afraid someone was gonna find out what happened down there at the creek last Friday."

Then he talked to the rest of us. "Freddy Wayne bet me and Jimmy that we was too scared to cross that bridge! Then he jeered and teased us so much we went ahead and tried. Worst of all was,"—he looked back to Freddy Wayne—"he didn't even try to help us when he seen we was in trouble. He just stood there half scared to death. Then he thought he would cover it all up by making Be More Happy look bad."

Bobby waited for a while and said, "If it weren't for that *crazy old man*, me and Jimmy would be dead right now!" Then he run on out of the clubhouse.

Nobody said nothing. What could you say about a thing like that?

Chapter 10

I hate to think about school starting, but come the end of July, I reckon it starts to work its way into everybody's thinking. I'd have to study on keeping it out of my mind.

The summer was really going by fast. After what happened up at the clubhouse a couple of weeks back, Freddy Wayne weren't so much of a problem. He kind of stuck close to his house. It made me feel sorry for Aunt Virginia, but I reckoned she knew how to take care of him.

They weren't a whole lot to do that time of the year. It was too hot for playing ball. A person could get a heatstroke. On really good days, Daddy would come home during the hot part of the day and take us all over to Lake Nixon to swim. That didn't happen too much, and this particular day it didn't. So I was left to find something to do for myself. I never heard tell of a bug hospital, but that's what I done.

Right before noon, Danny come home with a great big grasshopper what had a broken off leg. That was one of the sorriest things I ever seen. It couldn't hop worth a flit. That's when we come up with the idea to start a hospital.

After lunch, we rounded up all the things we thought we'd need for the job. We got all the little boxes we could find to use for beds. I gathered up toothpicks, string, tissues, and pins for various other remedies. Soap. We had our first disagreement about soap. That's understandable, though. Danny never could see no use for soap. The perfect spot for the hospital weren't hard to agree on. Down near the creek, where it goes by our house, just past the Indian's grave. It was shady and cool, there was plenty of water, and there was a graveyard, of sorts, nearby.

I reckon I ought to tell you about the Indian's grave. Right down the hill, where Garvin Street ends, there was a mound of dirt that we called the Indian's grave. That's what it looked like, and nobody knowed what it was or how it got there, so that's what we called it. There was plenty of times we talked about digging into it to see for sure was it a grave, but something always seemed to stop us. I can remember all of us standing around with our shovels ready, but somebody would remember that you shouldn't dig into a grave in broad daylight. To do it right, there had to be a full moon. Nobody argued with that. We decided to wait for the moon, but nobody seemed to know when it was gonna be full again. That's been a while ago, and us kids don't never take no notice of full moons these days.

Anyhow, that don't have nothing to do with our hospital. Me and Danny worked clearing out a spot so it would be clean and sanitary. We made some of the beds out of pine needles and the others was those little boxes that pills come in. Bobby come by and helped out. He went home and brought back a few things that was handy, some cotton and alcohol. It was decided that he would be the doctor, I would be the nurse, and Danny would be the ambulance driver. So me and Bobby did a little straightening around and devoted all our care to that poor grasshopper that started the whole thing by losing its leg.

It weren't long before Danny was back with enough patients to fill nearly every bed. There was crickets, worms, one lizard, and several beetles, all with different ailments. Some of them had to be kept in the boxes 'cause they didn't know how sick they was.

There are times when I can't believe how stupid I am! Bobby made a discovery when he was coming back to the hospital after supper. He seen Danny while he was out gathering up the poor little sick bugs, and found out what it was that was making them so sick.

When Bobby come back in to the hospital, I was down on my hands and knees looking under rocks and through dead leaves and brush. "What you looking for, Annie? he asked.

"Just look!" I said. "Ever last one of them crawled off while we was eating supper."

Bobby looked at all the empty beds and laughed. "Ain't no matter," he said. "I just seen Danny, and he's got plenty of replacements." Then he laughed again and said, "Heck, as long as we got Danny for a ambulance driver, we ain't never gonna run out of bugs to fix up."

I didn't catch on to what he was saying for a while, but when I did, it's for sure it weren't no laughing matter. Danny come back about that time with his little brown bag ambulance full of new *victim*s, and was right sorry he did.

I started kicking, and I didn't stop till there weren't no sign of a hospital. Then I did something I ain't proud of, but I was mad, and my tongue was hard to hold on to. "You're gonna be sorry, Danny!" I shouted.

"You wait! Some dark night, some big old bug is gonna come and pull one of your legs off."

Danny turned white, and I knew I was hitting my mark. "Just wait! You'll see how it feels." Then I run on up to the house. Bobby was laughing. I reckon he thought it was funny, but I didn't. Neither did Danny.

The next few days were long and hot. Weren't nothing happening. Me and Lou was sitting out on the front porch making up stories about the white, puffy clouds floating in the sky. Then it was, we seen the dust over the tree tops coming real slow up "H" Street. They was grading the roads. That was always something fun to watch.

By the time me and Lou got down there, everybody else was already sitting on that old broken off tree, watching the huge machines turning up the road. One thing for sure, that meant it would rain. It always rained right after they come to grade the roads, and what a muddy mess that made.

We all watched for a while, and then the man stopped and climbed down from the grader to get a drink from the big jug in the back of the truck that come with him. Soon as he stopped, them boys was all over that grader.

The man laughed when he come back and seen his grader crawling with boys. "Tell you what," he said. "Seeing as how this is the last time I'll be grading these roads, how would you like a little ride?"

Them boys about went out of their heads. They got their rides all right, so did me and Lou. It was scary, but it weren't half as scary as what we found out from the grader man. He told us the reason he weren't gonna be grading out our way anymore was 'cause the whole place, all the way to Mississippi Street, was gonna be in the city starting next month.

We all knew what that meant. We heard our folks talking about it often enough. It meant city schools. Weren't nothing wrong with the school we was going to. We all been going to Joe T. all our lives!

Now it was Freddy Wayne's turn to be Freddy Wayne again, and he proceeded to try and scare the pants off everyone, telling us how different the city schools was. He told about the rich people that went there, and how smart everybody was, so it would appear we was all a bunch of dummies.

I didn't want to hear no more, so I dropped behind the rest of them, pretending to study on a ant eating on a huckleberry. They was all gone soon enough and the woods was mine. I liked the woods best by myself, especially when I had something to think on.

I walked on through the woods, and before I knowed it I was up by the spring, there by my berry patch. Beats me how them boys still hadn't come on to it, but that was fine with me. I sat there staring into the water wondering why grownups always wanted to change things.

A voice interrupted my thinking. "Little people shouldn't have such big problems."

"Be More!" I said. "I didn't hear you come up."

"So I see," he said, sitting down beside me. "You have a problem, Annie?"

I threw a couple of rocks into the water before I answered. "Did you know they was gonna make this the city?"

"Is that so?" He sounded truly surprised. "Why does that trouble you?"

"I just don't like things to change," I said. "If we live in the city, that means we have to go to the city schools. I ain't never been to a city school."

He nodded like he understood. After a little while he said, "I went to a city school. Didn't seem too bad to me. Of course, that was a long, long time ago."

"I reckon they ain't all bad, but Freddy Wayne says the people who goes there is all rich and smart ..." I didn't finish, 'cause I was about to cry.

"When did Annie Marcus start listening to Freddy Wayne?" Be More asked as he stood up and walked over to the blackberry bushes.

"You know, Annie," he said thoughtfully, "whether you realize it or not, you are a very smart little girl. I don't know how you are with your studies, but you're smart about life, and that's what's important." He was searching the bush for berries. "You can't let people like Freddy Wayne bother you." He brought over a handful of berries, washed them off in the spring, and we shared them.

"And as for being rich," he said, "can you call anyone who has all these beautiful woods to roam around in poor? Money isn't what makes a person rich, Annie." For a while he didn't say nothing, and I looked up into them sad eyes. Then he slapped his hand on his leg and said, "Far as I'm concerned, you are the richest person I ever met."

We walked on down the hill together. Maybe Be More was right. Maybe I was rich. Anyhow, I always felt rich when Be More was around. But the smart part I was sure he was wrong about that. I ain't never been smart.

That night at supper, Lou was all bubbly and excited. She liked changes and was eager to start to the new school. I asked myself for the millionth time why I couldn't be like that. We were sisters, weren't we?

The next day was Saturday, and Daddy took us for a hike down by the river. Bobby come along, too. His mother was still sick so everybody in the neighborhood took turns taking him places. We was all having fun. Lou looked like she was kind of bored, but she had fun, too, I think. Then it was that I thought about what Be More was saying to me. I never once thought about not needing money to be rich, but there I was, walking along the river. They weren't nothing I'd rather be doing, and walking didn't cost nothing. I reckon I am rich!

Coming back, we walked down the railroad track, and Daddy showed us how to tell if a train was coming. I never knowed you could feel one coming before you could hear it. Of course, you have to be paying attention.

Right before we come to the road that crosses over back to the river, me and Bobby jumped like we was shot, and Daddy laughed.

"Shows who's paying attention," he said. Then he quickly got us all back away from the track. By the time we was safe away, we could hear the train coming. If Be More Happy thinks I'm smart, he ought to know my Daddy.

We got back home just in time to hear the program from the Boy's Club on the radio. Lou had gone down on Friday morning to sing, and they put the whole program on a tape recorder to put on the radio for Saturday. It was just like she was a movie star.

That night I had cause to be sorry for what I done to Danny the other day. Some people can do wrong things and it don't ever catch up with them, but not me.

Right before suppertime, Daddy asked who wanted to sleep out. That was great, and we all was thrilled. So Daddy set about putting up the tent out in the back yard. About the time the sun was going down, we built a fire and roasted hot dogs and marshmallows.

It was beautiful outside at night, what with the fire, the stars, the crickets chirping, and the whippoorwills.

Sometimes, I was scared at night, but not much. Danny was something else, though. He was always scared at night. On that night, I noticed he didn't seem to be having much fun. He wanted to sleep out, but then again, he didn't. We was sitting around the fire talking, when all of a sudden he starts to screaming like he was half-killed. Pretty near scared me and Lou out of our britches. Mama and Daddy, too, I guess. They come running around the house fast as they could.

Come to find out, a cricket had jumped on Danny's lap. Daddy and Mama couldn't figure anyone being scared of a cricket. I could. I knew what he was thinking, and it didn't make me feel good. I reckon I better learn to keep quiet when I'm mad.

Didn't none of us stay out. Danny's screaming had made me and Lou scared, too. Even if we hadn't been scared, I couldn't have no more fun, thinking about poor Danny half scared to death, and it being my fault. Be More may have been right about me being rich, but no, I don't reckon I'll ever call myself smart.

Chapter 11

Ain't it always so? When you think things is all settled, something comes along to spoil it all.

I wrestled with myself for the best part of two weeks over that city school business. One day I'd talk to Lou and she'd tell me how everything was just gonna be peachy creamy. Then them boys would come along and start telling their tales and there I'd be, right back where I started from. What Be More Happy said to me that day I was down to his house seemed to win out in the end. I reckon he knowed more than them boys, for sure.

I been going down to see Be More a lot more lately. Funny thing is, when I first went down to his house, I told myself it was 'cause he needed a friend. But I reckon things was changing. It was getting to be 'cause I needed a friend. Be More was a friend like I never had before. He listened to me when I talked. Not many people I knowed would do that. Lou did, but that was just 'cause she knowed if she didn't act like she was listening, she wouldn't have nobody to listen to her long tales in bed at night. Be More really listened and it made me feel important, like I was a real person.

Anyhow, that's what I was thinking on when I went out to the kitchen for breakfast that morning. I got myself a cup of cocoa and sat down to the table to wait for that eternal egg. Mama was looking out the kitchen window. Weren't nothing strange about that. It was when she blowed her nose real loud and turned around, I noticed they was something wrong. Her eyes was all puffy red like she been crying.

"Mama?" I said.

She turned around to the stove and cracked a egg in the skillet. "It's Bobby's mother, Annie," she said when she sat down. Then she didn't say nothing for a long time, she just kept on staring at the table cloth.

"What?" I asked. "Is she gonna have to go back to the hospital again."

"No, Annie," Mama said. "Bobby's mother died last night."

Mama sat there looking at my face like she was expecting something, but I didn't know what. I ain't never knowed nobody that died before, and I didn't know what to do. I found out a little while later, when I was in the front room. Lou had got up. I seen her going into the kitchen and heard her and Mama talking. I went over to the kitchen door and seen Lou in Mama's arms crying like a baby. I reckon I should of cried, too. I was crying on the inside, but there weren't no tears on my face.

The rest of that day was strange. Mama said we should stay close by and be quiet, so I didn't see nobody. I sure would of felt a whole lot better if I could of gone out in the woods. Right after lunch, Daddy come home. He hadn't been working, he'd been sitting with Bobby's daddy. He told Mama he was gonna rest for a while, then we'd all get cleaned up and go down there.

That day seemed like it was gonna go on forever. All I done was be quiet and listen to Mama and Lou sniffling in the kitchen. Mama was cooking some food to take down to their house. Danny was out on the front porch playing with his trucks. I figured I'd rather play with trucks than cry, so I went outside. I didn't play, though. I just sat on the porch and remembered Bobby's mother working in her rose garden.

Later on we went on down there. Nobody asked do you want to or nothing. We just went. If they'd of asked, I don't reckon I would of gone. Bobby was my friend, and I don't like to see nobody hurting.

Everybody in the neighborhood was down there. They was even some people I didn't know. It was a strange gathering. Everybody was acting happy, and talking, and laughing just like at a party. Even Bobby's daddy was laughing some. He looked sad, too, and sometimes when someone was talking to him his face would go blank and he would walk off like they wasn't even there.

Bobby was the one bothered me most. He just sat in that chair over in the corner of their front room, and ever so often, he'd take a picture out of his pocket and look at it. I reckon it was a picture of his mother.

Finally, I went on out on the porch. I couldn't take no more. Sad People trying to act like they weren't sad, and some who weren't sad trying to act like they was. Then there was poor Bobby, sitting there with his red, puffy eyes, staring at that picture. The porch was better. By myself was better. I wondered if maybe Be More Happy didn't have the right idea. Maybe he weren't so strange after all. Maybe lonely ain't as bad as some other things. I sat out there watching the lightning bugs and listening to that old whippoorwill. I could see Bobby sitting in that chair, but I didn't look but one time. Pretty soon I heard the screen door open, and Bobby come out and sat down next to me on the porch step. We didn't say nothing. I looked in his eyes for a long time, and I reckoned our eyes said everything we was feeling.

A little while later, Lou come out looking for me, to tell me it was time to go home. Bobby stood up and went on back in the house, nearly bumping into Lou, and not saying a word to her.

"What got into him?" Lou asked.

I didn't say nothing. I figured if she didn't know, telling wouldn't make no difference.

The funeral was the day after next. Another one of those things where nobody asked if a person wanted to go. We just all went. It weren't as happy as the gathering down to Bobby's house the other night, more like someone told everybody to be sad, so they was. I didn't like none of it and was ready for it all to be over. At the last, when everybody got in line to have a look in the coffin, I stayed where I was. So did Danny. Lou marched right up there crying and carrying on just like everybody else. I didn't like her very much that day.

The next week was awful. Seemed to me I was just plain in a bad mood. I didn't even go outside, just moped around the house all day not doing nothing. Not talking to nobody.

It was Friday afternoon, and I was in my room counting the flowers on the wallpaper. There was a knock on the door and Mama said, "Annie, someone out in the front yard wants to see you."

Yuck! Them boys again. I reckon Lou asked them to come and ask me to play ball. She couldn't stand having me around the house all the time. That was her territory. The woods was mine, but even the woods weren't the same those days.

"You hear me, Annie?" Mama asked.

I figured I better go on out. It would be better than having Mama hollering at the door all afternoon.

Was I surprised! It weren't them boys this time. It was Be More Happy. He was sitting right there on my front porch, big as life, drinking a glass of iced tea.

I went out and sat down next to him.

"I've been missing you," he said.

I looked at him and then looked away. "I just ain't been feeling like coming out in the woods."

"You look sad," he said looking straight at me.

I knowed Be More knew what was wrong, probably better than I did. "I reckon I don't exactly know what's wrong." We sat for a while not saying nothing. "I got sad when Bobby's mama died and I just stayed sad. I ain't never knowed nobody that died before." Be More was listening, and it felt good, so I went on. "I didn't like seeing Bobby hurting so bad, and they weren't nothing I could do to make him feel good.

"At the funeral, everybody was crying and carrying on, everyone but me. I reckon everybody thought I didn't like Bobby's mother or something, but I did. I liked her a lot. I just didn't have no tears." I stopped to think for a while. "Why didn't I have tears, Be More?"

He sighed long and deep and said, "Annie, every one of us reacts differently to certain situations. You don't seem to me to be the crying type, but I'm sure you hurt on the inside as much as anybody. You just express it differently." He looked at me to see if I was understanding and I reckon he seen I weren't 'cause he went on explaining.

"You see, you decided to punish yourself instead of crying, and you did that by taking yourself away from the things you loved most. Your woods and your friends." He put his finger under my chin and raised up my face so we was looking right at each other.

"Can you see what I'm saying to you, Annie? Punishing yourself won't bring back Bobby's mother. That's been tried before, and it doesn't work."

I knowed he was talking about hisself then, and I asked, "Is that what you tried to do, Be More?"

He looked off into the woods with them big sad eyes and said slowly, "I tried, Annie. I tried for years, but it didn't work. Maybe we'd both be better off if we could just cry it out."

We sat for a long time thinking on that, and then I asked, "Be More, Preacher Driggers kept saying that Bobby's mother weren't dead, that she had just gone away. What do you reckon he meant by that?"

I could tell that all this weren't making Be More too happy, but he answered anyway. "People don't ever really die, Annie. At least, that's the way I see it. Their bodies die, but their spirits keep on living. Bobby's mother is probably somewhere working in a rose garden right now." He looked at my face to see if I believed what he was saying. I didn't have no cause not to. Then he went on, but I felt like he weren't talking to me no more, but to hisself. He sounded far away.

"It's the ones that are left behind that die. They die a little every time they hear a little girl giggle, and know they'll never hear their own child laugh again. They die a little when they see a mother and her daughter walking down the street together and know ..." He didn't say no more. He was looking off into the woods like he was a hundred miles away. There was the same hurt on his face I seen on Bobby's down to his house that night.

I put my hand on his. If only I knew how to take hurt away from people! First Bobby and now Be More. And *I* done it to Be More. I made him think about the things that make him sad. Then it was the tears came. I hate to cry! But seeing Be More hurting like that, I couldn't hold it back no more.

It was my tears that brung Be More back from wherever he was to the front porch. He looked surprised to see me crying.

"What's this? Annie Marcus crying?" he said.

"I'm sorry, Be More," I said, trying to hide my tears. "You looked so sad, like you was hurting on the inside."

"It's all right," he said. "You cry all you want, but Annie, you don't need to ever cry for me. You above all people." He took his big handkerchief from his pocket and started wiping my face.

"Let me tell you, Annie, I've been dying inside for so many years now, I don't know what kept me hanging on to life. I guess I was dead inside. Then a certain freckle-faced little girl started coming around, and little by little, Annie, you have brought this old man back to life." He put his hands on my shoulders and smiled into my face. A smile that was full of life and love. "Don't ever cry for me. You are the one who has given me back my life."

Be More left not long after that, but not before he told me about Lou. It was her that went to Be More's place and told him I was out-of-sorts. I reckon I don't know as much about people as I like to think I do.

That ended up being a real good day. I was proud that Lou weren't scared to go down to Be More's house. Sometimes I get upset with her prissy ways, but all in all, I reckon she's a good sister to have. Then there was Be More's visit. Without asking no questions at all, I learned more about him that day than I ever had. What I learned made me sorry for him, but that smile on his face made up for it. I'd be remembering that smile for a long time to come.

Chapter 12

The Labor Day Picnic, and we was late! My Mama and her fried chicken. It had to be just so, or she was a nervous wreck.

Finally, when Mama's chicken was *just so*, we all piled into the car and headed for Boyle Park. We was gonna be the last ones there for sure. And we was.

When we got there everybody was gathered around Be More Happy's old black truck. The watermelon! I jumped out of the car soon as it stopped and run on over there. Sure enough, there was our melon. A big one, too. I thanked Be More with my smile. There weren't no smile on his face, but I could tell he was glad he done it.

Everybody knowed Be More weren't the sociable type, and it didn't seem to bother nobody. He stood off by hisself most of the time. Once in a while I'd see someone like Doc Elder or Mr. Weaver wander over to him and say a few words, but Be More only nodded and looked uncomfortable. I tried staying with him for a while, but that weren't no good. He seen what I was doing and told me to run on and have fun. I knowed they weren't no use to argue.

There was Bobby! The Labor Day Picnic was something that happened every year. Everybody in the neighborhood met at Boyle Park and had one big get-together before school started. I didn't expect to see Bobby there that year. He had been staying with his aunt over across the river ever since his mother died. But I reckon he had to come home sometime, and with school starting the next day, he didn't have a whole lot of choice. He looked good. Cleaner than I seen him in a while, but that's what aunts is good for … getting things clean.

"Bobby!" I hollered, and he motioned for me to come on over to where he was by that little lake.

"What you been up to, Annie?" he said.

"Ain't nothing to be up to around here. You know that." I didn't know nothing else to say. Neither did he. We was just standing there chucking rocks in the lake when Freddy Wayne and Jimmy come over. Freddy Wayne's been a whole lot quieter lately, but he weren't about to pass up a chance to make someone feel bad.

"Lookie, lookie, Jimbo," he said with that real sickly giggle. "What's this we got here? Two little lovebirds?"

Bobby's face turned so red it was near to purple, and his hands was clenched in a fist.

"You better hush your mouth, Freddy Wayne," I said. I was mad all right, but more than that, I was scared Bobby was gonna start hitting.

"I ain't done nothing," Freddy Wayne said, and held his hands up acting like he was afraid I was gonna hit him. "Nothing but notice that you two seem to enjoy each other's company a awful lot." Then he giggled again.

Jimmy sniffled so as he could giggle too. Only he never got to, 'cause it was about that time that Junior walked up and put his arms acrost Freddy Wayne and Jimmy's shoulders, and said real sweet like, "Sure is a nice picnic, ain't it boys?" Freddy Wayne's face turned red and Junior went on, "We ain't gonna have no fighting today, not with school starting tomorrow." He seen Freddy Wayne weren't taking kindly to his advice, and patted them both on the back a little harder than he needed to, and said, "I mean, wouldn't it be a shame to go to school on the first day with a busted lip? What do you say, Freddy Wayne?"

Freddy Wayne didn't have time to say nothing, 'cause Uncle Ariel was whistling to call everyone to eat.

We had everything to eat that you'd expect to have at a picnic. There was fried chicken, potato salad, deviled eggs, corn relish, cakes and pies, soda pop, and of course, watermelon.

I fixed a plate and carried it over to Be More. He was sitting in the back of his truck and watching what all was going on like someone might watch a picture show.

"You having fun, Be More?" I asked.

"Nicest picnic I've ever been to," he said, and he looked like he really meant it. I don't mean to give you the idea that he looked happy or nothing. Fact of the matter was, he didn't look happy at all.

"You don't look happy, Be More," I said. "Is something troubling you?"

Then it was, his face went blank, like I weren't there, like no one weren't there. I wondered if I would ever learn what I could or couldn't say to Be More Happy.

I looked down at the ground and said, "I reckon I better go and let you eat. Looks like Mama's got mine ready, too." Then I walked on over to the tables where all the food was spread out. I think I heard Be More say thanks for the plate, but I don't know for sure. I looked back once, and he was eating, but he didn't even look happy about that.

It appeared that eating calmed down some certain people, or most likely it was what Junior done before we ate. Anyhow, after everybody was finished, all us kids played baseball, and nobody said nothing mean to nobody. Freddy Wayne even had a kind word for Danny after the little rascal made a home run by sliding into the plate, right between Charles Edward's legs.

While we was playing ball, I seen Be More take the watermelon out of the back of his truck and put it on the table. Then he stood and watched us play ball for a while. Pretty soon, our eyes met each other, and it was like we was talking, only they weren't no words. His eyes was telling me that he was going home, and my eyes was telling him it was okay, I understood.

Doc Elder seen what went between me and Be More and looked like he wanted to say something to me about it, but instead, marked it up in his head for later. Unfortunately, Doc Elder weren't the only one what seen it. Freddy Wayne come walking over to where I was standing watching Be More drive away.

"You don't look out, you're gonna be just like that crazy old man before long," he said, and started polishing his glasses.

I looked at him long and hard before I said, "I can't think of no one I'd rather be like."

"Y'all gonna play ball or what?" Charles Edward hollered.

Freddy Wayne just spit on the ground and turned around and walked off.

"Don't let him bother you none, Sugar," Junior said and put his arm acrost my shoulders. "Come on now, everyone's waiting to play ball."

Bobby looked like he wanted to say something, too, but thought better of it. I reckon he didn't like being called a lovebird. Can't say as I cared too much for it, but Bobby was the only one of them boys worth being friends with, except for Junior and Danny of course. Least ways, I had hopes for Danny.

We kept on playing ball till Daddy come over and asked us if we was ready to eat a piece of watermelon. I tell you, I ain't never tasted no better watermelon nowhere. Daddy says things always tastes better when you grow them yourself. I can't actually say I growed it, but I helped with it from time it was just a regular melon till it growed to be a giant. They weren't nothing Be More Happy couldn't do! I was certain of that.

Some of them boys was a real mystery. There they was, eating a watermelon growed by that *crazy old man* and loving it. I just wished they'd care that much for Be More. Sometimes, seemed like all they wanted was what they could get out of a person.

When we finished our watermelon, we was too full for playing any more ball, so we sat in the shade, and unfortunately the subject of school come up. Soon as Freddy Wayne took off his glasses and started polishing on them, I knowed he was gonna say something snotty.

He looked over at me and Danny and Jerry and said, "You little ones ready for that big old city school tomorrow?"

"Let them be, Freddy Wayne," Lou said. "There ain't nothing to be scared of."

"Scared of?" Danny asked like he never thought of that before. Only I knowed he had.

Then Billy spoke up. "Me and Jerry been to plenty of city schools. They ain't no different than any other school." He stopped to think for a minute. "Sometimes they is bigger, that's all."

"And sometimes the studies is harder," Charles Edward put in. Studies was always hard for Charles Edward.

Freddy Wayne opened up his mouth to say something, but Junior got there first. "Reckon we won't know a whole lot about what city schools is and city schools ain't till tomorrow. So ain't no use to talk about it." He looked over to Freddy Wayne and grinned real sweet. "Ain't that right, Freddy Wayne?"

He didn't get no answer. Freddy Wayne stomped on off and started helping Aunt Virginia to pack up so as they could leave.

I hadn't seen Bobby say nothing much to nobody for most of the day. It weren't clear to me if it was 'cause of what Freddy Wayne said, or if he was still hurting for his mother. Whatever, just about all he done was stand and chuck rocks into the water.

I hated it when time come to go home, 'cause I knowed then we'd be getting ready for school the next day. Anyhow, it didn't matter what I wanted, we was going home.

Doc Elder come to me before he left. "Annie," he started, and I thought for a while he forgot what he was gonna say. I felt embarrassed for him. Then he went ahead, like as if he just made up his mind about something real important. "You tell Be More Happy that was the sweetest watermelon I ever tasted."

I smiled real big. "Okay, Doc Elder. I'll be sure to tell him."

Then he walked on over to his car, and he turned around to wave goodbye before he got in. I had a feeling that watermelon weren't what he had in mind to talk about.

Later on at home, me and Lou helped Mama clean things up in the kitchen, and Mama explained all the good that was gonna come from going to a city school.

"You're gonna be associating with a better class of people," she said, and her eyes sparkled when she stopped to think on it. "Maybe you'll learn to quit with all the *reckons* and *ain'ts*. I wish I'd of learned that when I was younger."

That was when I left. To think, I'd even have to talk different! I wondered if Freddy Wayne knowed about that.

Lou didn't seem to mind. Sometimes I thought Lou and Mama was one in the same person. Only Mama was trying to make Lou into what she always wanted to be, and wasn't.

I decided that would be a good time for me to take that piece of watermelon we saved for Be More on down to his place. It weren't just the watermelon, though. I needed to talk to someone, and if I weren't wrong about it, so did Be More.

When I got down to his place, Be More was busy raking up some leaves around his house, and I thought how it wouldn't be long before all the leaves started to fall. Fall sure was a pretty time of the year. If it weren't for school starting then, I reckon I'd like it.

"I brung you a piece of your watermelon, Be More," I said as I walked into his yard.

"Why hello, Annie," he said, leaning his rake up against the house. As he took the watermelon from my hands, he said, "You didn't have to do that."

"It was your watermelon, and I reckon you ought to get at least one piece," I said. "Everybody said to tell you it was delicious, and Doc Elder said it was the sweetest he ever tasted."

"Is that so?" he said in a way I could tell he weren't sad no more. "Maybe you and I should go into the watermelon business. What do you think?"

I laughed. I knowed he was pulling my leg. "Sorry you had to leave so soon, Be More," I said, "but it was nice of you to come."

He just nodded to that, and I figured by the look on his face I better change the subject.

"School starts tomorrow," I said.

I reckon Be More heard the dread in my voice. He looked at me concerned-like and said, "Let me put this watermelon inside, then we can sit over on the bench and talk." Walking on off into the house, he hollered back, "Can I get you something to drink?"

"No thanks," I answered. After that picnic, I didn't think I'd ever want to eat or drink again.

Be More come back out, and we sat over there on the bench around the tree and talked for a long time.

"You're still worried about going to a new school?" he asked as he sat down on the bench.

"I reckon I am," I sighed. "Them boys keep saying terrible things. Mama tries to make us feel good about it, but what she says don't make me feel good."

Be More nodded like he knowed just what I was talking about. "You won't have any problems, Annie. I wish I could make you believe that."

"I wish I was like Lou," I said, more to myself than to Be More. "She won't have no problems. You can be sure of that."

Be More frowned. "I think you're nice just the way you are." He stood up real fast and said, "Wait here a minute, I want to show you something." And he stalked off over to his tool shed.

After a while, he come back carrying a little nail keg like it was real heavy. When he got over to the bench, he turned up the keg and dumped it out on the ground. I never seen anything like it. They must have been a million crystals right there on the ground in front of me, sparkling in the sun like diamonds.

"Be More," I whispered. "They're beautiful."

His face looked happy even if he weren't smiling. "I've been collecting those for many, many years, Annie." Then he looked at me like he was about to challenge me to jump over the moon or something. "I want you to do something for me." He got down on his knees and spread the crystals out. "I want you to pick out the prettiest one."

I looked at his face to see if he was kidding, but he weren't. On my hands and knees, I searched through them, but they was all so pretty. Finally, I gave up. "They're all pretty, Be More."

He sat back down on the bench, took hold of my shoulders, and looked me right in the eye. "People are just like those crystals, Annie. There are no two alike, and each one is special for a different reason. Do you understand what I'm saying to you?"

"I understand," I said. "I should be proud to be me and not want to be like anyone else."

"That's right. The world could use more sparkly-eyed little Annies. And here you are, wanting to change the only one it has." He smiled at me. "You just be yourself at school tomorrow, and everyone will love you."

Be More Happy was the best thing that ever happened to me. I didn't worry no more about school. The thing that bothered me right then was that Be More always helped me so much, and I didn't never do nothing for him. I'd have to do something about that.

Chapter 13

I was already up and dressed when Mama come in to wake us up. Lou was sleeping like a baby and weren't at all easy to get out of the bed. I don't know how she did it. Seemed to me I was awake most of the night. When I talked to Be More Happy yesterday, I didn't think I'd worry anymore. But there's just something about the dark that brings out ever little worry a person can think on. At least, that's the way it is for me.

Lou finally got up and put on her new pleated wool skirt and white long-sleeved blouse. I reckoned as how she was gonna be sorry for that and told her as much.

"You're gonna be sorry for that before the day's done," I said to her. "It's gonna be getting hot."

"I reckon … I mean, probably so, but I want to make a good impression," she answered back, and looked at my dress but didn't say nothing. So what if it was plain? Leastways, it was cool.

At breakfast, nobody said nothing about the new school. Mama talked about how good we all looked, and Daddy said it sure was nice to have everybody to breakfast at the same time. Other than that, things was just like always, and I couldn't understand how it could seem so normal when the whole world was turned upside down.

Soon as we was all ready and had our lunchboxes packed, we left to go on over to Aunt Dorothy's house. It felt good to be outside walking through the woods. There was a mockingbird singing in a tall pine tree. I wished I could take on off through the woods and just foller him around all day. Then it was, I seen something sparkling in the dirt off to one side of the path. A crystal! I remembered what me and Be More talked about, bent down to pick it up, and whispered, "Thanks, Be More."

"Annie, get out of that dirt before you get yourself dirty," Lou said.

I put the crystal in my pocket. Things wasn't so bad after all. It was a beautiful sunny day, and that crazy mockingbird follered us all the way to Aunt Dorothy's house, singing its head off the whole way.

Over to Aunt Dorothy's house, things was strange. Them boys was all there, but they was unusual quiet. Aunt Virginia had come over with Freddy Wayne and Jimmy. She was gonna take Junior and Freddy Wayne up to the junior high school, and Aunt Dorothy was gonna take the rest of us to our school. Freddy Wayne was the strangest one of all. He didn't have nothing to say to nobody. I seen then the reason why he was trying so hard to scare everyone. He wanted us all to be as scared as he was. I almost felt sorry for him while I watched them driving on off down the road.

We all piled into Aunt Dorothy's car like a bunch of sardines, and it weren't but a few minutes till we was pulling up in front of a neat-looking yellow brick building with a flagpole standing right out in front. Fair Park Elementary School!

Everybody on the playground stared while we got out of the car one at a time. I reckon it looked like they weren't gonna be no end to us. We all walked up that big sidewalk, right on through the front door, and up the steps to the office with Aunt Dorothy leading the way. A real nice lady with gray hair and twinkling eyes met us. Aunt Dorothy talked to her for a while, and then the lady come over and introduced herself to us.

"Children," she said as we all watched Aunt Dorothy leave, "I'm Mrs. Reed, the principal of Fair Park." That was strange. She didn't look mean enough to be a principal. "Now, you're going to have to help me with your names for a while," she went on. "I'm sure you will love Fair Park, and we're all going to love you." Then she called out our names and gave us a card we was supposed to give to our teachers. "Follow me," she said and started off down the hall.

Danny was the first one left off in his class. He looked so alone I almost cried for him. Then she took Bobby and Billy to their class. Both of them was in the fifth grade and that was upstairs. They liked that, but they didn't like being left up there alone with that strange redheaded teacher. Lou, Charles Edward, and Jimmy was next. They was all sixth graders, and I reckon they figured they was too old to act scared, but Jimmy was having a hard time hiding it. He weren't use to being separated from Freddy Wayne. Me and Jerry was last, and I was glad of that. At least, I knowed where everybody was. If I could remember.

Me and Jerry was in the fourth grade. Mrs. Reed explained that the fourth grade ate lunch and had recess with the fifth and sixth grades, so we would see our friends in a little while. That made me feel good for us, but bad for poor little Danny, all alone in the second grade.

Things turned out really good. It all started when I come across that crystal in the woods. I was ready for anything after that, and they was a lot of different things to be ready for. But I was learning real fast that different weren't always bad. To start off with, there was riding with Aunt Dorothy instead of that smelly old school bus. Then there was Mrs. Reed, a sweet little old lady, instead of Mr. Jones, a scary sort who most always carried a paddle with him. Fair Park was gonna be okay!

The first recess went by pretty good. My class chose up sides for playing chase. I reckon city folks don't have a whole lot of call to run, 'cause I outrun all of them by a long ways. Jerry had brung a whole pocketful of marbles, so he didn't have no trouble finding someone to play with. I seen Lou sitting on the ground talking to a bunch of girls, and then they all got up and started jumping around, doing cheers. I knowed what that meant, she'd be wanting to be a cheerleader. She'd do it, too! Charles Edward and the rest of them boys was all playing football and didn't look to be having no problems.

I liked my teacher. She smelled like roses and spoke very softly. The classroom was clean. At Joe T. things was clean, but they never really looked it. Mama said it was 'cause of them big black stoves in every room. They weren't one in my new school. It had them radiators like in the buildings uptown.

When it was time to eat lunch, we all washed our hands, and I was the last one to go back to the cloak room to get my lunchbox. It was kind of dark in there, and I heard noise coming from over in the corner. I walked over there and seen it was that little black-haired girl crying.

"Is something the matter?" I asked.

"You won't tell Miss Tanner?" she sniffled.

"I don't reckon ... why?" I didn't understand how anyone could be scared of Miss Tanner.

"I lost my lunch money. So I'm just gonna stay in here till after lunch," she said.

The rest of the class had gone on to the cafeteria. I looked at Miss Tanner sitting at her desk and wondered if a person really would get in trouble for losing something. I decided the little black-haired girl must be wrong. Nobody that smelled like roses could be mean.

I took her hand and said, "Come on. If I know my Mama, they is enough food for three people in this here lunchbox."

She follered me on out the door, eyeing my lunchbox all the way to the cafeteria. We shared my lunch, and I found out her name was Zola Ann, and she had just moved to town from up north. That explained why she talked so funny, and I reckon her strange ideas about people getting in trouble, too. She was a Yankee!

We went on out on the playground after we was finished. I seen the boys playing football, so we stopped to watch for a minute. Putting my hand in my pocket, I felt that crystal I found in the woods that morning and brung it out to show to Zola Ann.

About that time, some boy I never seen before come up and said, "What's that you got, girl?" Then he snatched my crystal and run off with it. I reckon he was right sorry he done that, 'cause it weren't ten seconds till he had Charles Edward, Bobby, Jimmy, and Jerry after him.

Bobby brung me back my crystal, and Zola Ann just stood there with her mouth open. "Who were they?" she asked as soon as she found her voice.

"Charles Edward is my cousin," I said. "The rest is just friends what live out by me."

We stood and watched the game a little while longer. I noticed that Zola Ann was mostly watching Bobby, and I didn't know why, but I didn't like her looking at him the way she was.

"Come on, Zola Ann," I said. "Let's see if we can play chase."

By the time the day was over, I was in love with Fair Park Elementary. The kids weren't no different. But the school was. All to the good, though. Joe T. was a real good school, but Fair Park had won me over all in one day.

The thing I liked best was that it was so clean. And only one person was the reason for that. He was a giant black man by the name of Ethan. Everywhere you went in that school, there was Ethan, whistling up a storm and pushing a broom or mop around. And always, that dust cloth hanging out his back pocket. The whole place sparkled and smelled like clean laundry hanging in a piney woods.

When the day was over we all piled into Aunt Dorothy's car again. She had to go to the store up to Hillcrest, and while we was up there, she bought us all a jelly doughnut at the bakery. That made everything perfect.

As it happened, Danny made out okay. I reckon I should of knowed he would. He was the easiest person in the world to get on with. Daddy always said he'd probably grow up to be president some day. It appeared he didn't have no likes or dislikes of his own. If he run across someone what liked to eat mud pies, then mud pies was his favorite food, too. He didn't never have no trouble making friends.

Listening to all them talking, I wondered why we had all been so worried. I knowed all along Danny made friends easy, if I'd of just stopped to think about it. He always did. And I knowed them boys was better at sports than most. That come in handy for making friends. Lou never had no problems with people, either. While I was thinking on all that, I seen the reason why we had all been so scared, driving up behind us. Freddy Wayne! I think that boy must of been half devil.

I reckon the happiest part of the whole day for me was when Aunt Virginia stopped to let Junior out, and Freddy Wayne hollered out the car window and asked how we liked the big city school. When he seen how happy we all was, he was downright disappointed.

Walking back through the woods to our house, I seen Be More Happy sitting on a stump. I reckon he come up to wait for us, to see how things went, 'cause he was quite a ways from his place.

"Be More!" I hollered and waved. Lou and Danny waved to him, too, but they went on home.

"Be More!" I said again as I run over to where he was sitting, "You was right! I didn't have no trouble. None of us did. And Fair Park is a really nice place."

He kind of chuckled and held up his hand. "Slow down, Annie. I want to hear all about it."

So I told him everything. I told him about how pretty and clean Fair Park was, about Mrs. Reed and her twinkling eyes, Miss Tanner's soft voice and her smelling just like roses, and all about Ethan keeping the place so clean. I could of gone on for hours.

"Did you make any new friends?" he interrupted.

"Oh, yeah, I was coming to that," I said, taking note that his eyes was happy. "Zola Ann. She's new, too. We shared my lunch 'cause she lost her lunch money."

Be More slapped his knee. "Didn't I tell you if you would just be yourself you would be okay?"

That reminded me of the crystal, and I pulled it out of my pocket. "Look, Be More," I said. "I found this on the way to school this morning." Then I ducked my head and said, "Every time I got scared, I'd feel it in my pocket, and remember what you said. Then everything would be okay again." I held it out to him and asked, "Would you take it and put it in your collection?"

He just stared at it and then asked, "Are you sure that's what you want, Annie? Wouldn't you rather keep it and start your own collection?"

"No, Be More. I want you to have this one, it's special," I answered him.

He took it and put it in his pocket like it embarrassed him. Then I went on telling him about school, and he listened like he really was interested.

Finally, I said that I best be getting on home before Mama come after me with a switch.

"I'm glad everything worked out all right for you, Annie," he said before he started on off. "You take care, and if you need anything, you know where to find me."

I didn't really have to know where to find him, 'cause anytime I ever needed him, he was right there. It was spooky in a way, but nice. Friends is nice to have.

Supper lasted a long time that night, 'cause each one of us had to tell everything that happened at school. I was right about Lou. She was wanting to be a cheerleader. Danny thought it would be real nice if he could be on the football team and didn't take kindly to Daddy explaining that he weren't quite big enough.

Later that night, in bed, Lou left off talking about her singing career and talked about cheerleading, just like I knowed she would. While she talked, I thought about a lot of things. I thought about school, Be More Happy, Miss Tanner, but most of all, Zola Ann and the way she looked at Bobby. I still didn't know why I didn't like that. It just made me feel uncomfortable.

Chapter 14

Like I said before, Fall is sure a pretty time of the year around here. The days are nice and cool, and sometimes the air is so brisk it almost hurts to breathe. The colors is the best part, though. All my favorites. Yellow. Orange. Brown. Red. Everything was just plain pretty.

It'd been over a month since school started, and you'd of thought we had been going to Fair Park all our lives. All them boys ended up on the football team. All but Jerry and Danny, they was too little. And you might know, Lou got to be cheerleader.

Having a sister that was a cheerleader come in handy. We got to go to all the games, and sometimes I helped out if one of the cheerleaders needed someone to catch her when she turned a flip. Boys was always buying Lou hot dogs and things like that, and she was real good about sharing with me.

Sometimes, though, as good a school as Fair Park was, I still missed Joe T. Last Saturday, Daddy took us out to climb Pinnacle Mountain, and we drove right by Joe T. Lou said she didn't miss nothing about it. I kind of had a feeling like I turned my back on a old friend. But I reckoned good old Joe T. could get on without me.

Anyhow, school had been going on long enough that Saturdays was getting to be real special days. On that particular Saturday, I didn't want to do nothing but mess around in the woods. I'd kick up a few leaves, turn over a couple of rocks, and maybe by lunchtime I'd be in a better mood.

I ain't easy to get mad, but what happened at school on Friday was enough to make a preacher cuss. There was a whole school meeting to give out the parts for the Thanksgiving Program. I don't reckon, if I live to be a hundred years old, I'll ever understand why it is that just 'cause a person is quiet, people think she's stupid.

Set design! I didn't want to design no set. Everybody I knowed got a part in the program. Lou was gonna sing a song, Danny was the little Indian boy that opened and closed the curtain on the stage, and the rest of them boys was either Pilgrim or Indian children. Then there was Bobby! Bobby was the Pilgrim father, and you might guess who the Pilgrim mother was. Zola Ann!

Now what can I say about that? I reckon the look on Zola Ann's face said it all. She was tickled pink. Only good thing happened the whole day was when Bobby asked if he could switch parts with someone. Said he didn't want to be no Pilgrim father. Zola Ann's face fell so fast it nearly hit the floor. It didn't stay there long though, 'cause Mrs. Reed announced that there was to be no switching parts around.

I didn't reckon I should of felt the way I did. Zola Ann was my best friend, but Bobby was a friend of a different sort. That's part of what bothered me, not knowing what sort of friend Bobby was. I just knowed he was different from other boys.

That afternoon, Miss Tanner tried to explain what an important job set design was. She said that I was chosen for it because I was good at art. I knowed better. They was just afraid I'd mess their old program up by not talking loud enough or something.

I'd been sitting on that old log for nearly a hour thinking on all that and watching the squirrels gathering acorns and hickory nuts. Finally, I got so mad just thinking on it, I hollered out as loud as I could, "*I can talk loud when I want to!*"

I nearly swallowed my tongue when a soft voice behind me said, "I believe you can."

Be More Happy! No matter how good of friends we got to be, he could still scare the pants off me.

"Be More," I said. "You scared me half to death!"

"I didn't scare you nearly as much as you scared the poor little squirrels. Look here." He stooped down where they had been. "They even left behind their acorns."

"That's too bad," I said, and I reckon I sounded just like I felt.

"What's troubling you, Annie?" he asked.

I started walking back and forth, kicking up leaves. I don't recall ever being so mad about nothing. At last, I blurted out, "You and all your talk about crystals, when all the time I ain't nothing but a plain old brown rock."

Then I went on and told him the whole story. I didn't say nothing about Zola Ann and Bobby, though. How could I explain something to someone else that I didn't understand myself?

We walked on off through the woods. Be More didn't say nothing for a long time. Finally, when we come back to where we started, he asked, "Everybody got their part in the program typed up on a piece of paper, I guess?"

I nodded my head, feeling sorry for myself, and said, "Everybody but me."

He looked at me then with one eyebrow raised. "You didn't get anything?"

"Only Mrs. Reed's book," I pouted.

"Oh, I see. You only got the whole program, and everybody else got their own part." He weren't laughing, but I still felt like he was teasing me.

"Answer a question for me, Annie," he went on. "What would happen if one of the Pilgrims or Indians got sick and couldn't do their part?"

That was something I hadn't thought on. Maybe someone would get sick. Maybe I could do their part for them.

As it happened, me and Be More weren't thinking the same. When I didn't answer, he answered his own question. "Probably they would just work around it and do without that part of the program," he said.

I sure was glad I didn't say what I had been thinking. Else right about then I would of been real embarrassed.

Then Be More asked, "What do you suppose would happen if you got sick and couldn't get the set ready?"

I seen what he was getting at. All them other parts in the program could be done without, but not mine. For the first time, I was glad for having set design.

"I reckon I was wrong, huh, Be More?"

"Not wrong, Annie. Sometimes it's hard for people to see themselves the way others see them," he said.

"You mean like thinking you're a brown rock when you're really a crystal?" We both laughed.

"That's exactly right, my little crystal," he answered.

Then we started talking about set design for the program. Be More had a lot of good ideas, and talking helped me to think of things, too.

"Miss Tanner said I could use all the paints and stuff I want," I said. "I wish I could paint a tree like that one to put up on the stage." We both sat and looked at the beautiful yellow sweetgum tree. Be More's eyes was twinkling. I didn't hardly ever see them sad and lonely no more.

"Too bad we didn't grow some pumpkins," Be More said. "They would come in handy for your program."

"Yeah," I answered back. The woods was working their magic on both of us. We just sat, looking at the beautiful colors and watching the squirrels. They had finally come back after the acorns that I scared them away from a few minutes ago.

After a while, I said, "Reckon I better get on home. Mama's going up to Hillcrest this afternoon."

Be More just nodded like he didn't want to break the wood's magic spell.

"Thanks for making me see things right, Be More," I said. "You always make me feel good about things. Know what my Daddy would say? He'd say you'd make a good politician."

Then it was like a black cloud passed over Be More Happy's face. It was hard to tell if he was the same person I'd just been talking to. While I stood there looking into his eyes, they seemed to get even darker, and his face looked pained.

"Go on home, Annie," he said in a voice I could just barely hear.

I started on off without saying nothing. Then feeling ashamed of myself, I turned around to say goodbye. Be More weren't there. He weren't nowhere to be seen. Do I have to tell you I run all the way home? Didn't make no matter how good I got to know him, deep inside I was still scared.

We went on up to Hillcrest right after lunch. Mama went to the grocery store. Daddy give us a dollar this time, 'cause next week was Halloween, and we needed to get masks and things.

After we was finished, me and Danny still had ten cents left, so we decided to go over to the bakery and get a jelly doughnut. Just when we was coming out of the bakery, Daddy come out of the store next door. It was Mr. Cox's appliance store, the one with the television in the window. Try as we might, we couldn't get him to say nothing about what he was doing in there, but he had that look on his face like to say, "You'll find out."

We found out all right! No sooner did we get home than Mr. Cox pulled up to the house in his truck. A television! Daddy bought a television.

They worked the rest of the afternoon putting up the antenna and trying to get a picture to come in. They weren't nothing on but a test pattern. Mr. Cox said the programs would start coming in around six o'clock.

Soon as it was all hooked up and adjusted, Danny sat hisself down in front of it and didn't move. Even Lou seemed excited. We ate dinner early that night so we'd be sure to be finished before six o'clock.

I hadn't been able to get too awful excited about the television, 'cause I was still wondering about Be More Happy. Daddy noticed this and asked, "What's the matter, Annie? Why aren't you as excited as everybody else?"

Lou answered for me, "She's just disappointed 'cause she didn't get a part in the Thanksgiving Program at school."

"You shouldn't feel bad, Annie," Mama said. "Everybody can't sing and do things like that." Then she smiled real sweet at Lou.

Daddy seen that and said, "Is singing all they're gonna do? Why couldn't she have done something else?"

"There's lots of other things," Lou said. "I think they was just afraid Annie wouldn't talk loud enough."

That's when I left the table. Nobody said nothing about set design. And if I was such a bright sparkly crystal, why couldn't anyone else see it?

We watched television that night. It was just like having a picture show all to ourselves. I don't care much for fighting, though, and that was about all that was on.

Later on, in bed, Lou talked her head off about her song, and her this, and her that. I didn't listen, though. I was still trying to figure out what I said that made Be More act the way he did. Was it talking about my Daddy, or saying he'd be a good politician? That's all I said, but why would either one upset him so much? Be More Happy was such a mystery!

The next morning things seemed a little bit better, and before the day was over, it was a whole lot better. We went to church, and soon as I was finished helping to clean up after that delicious chicken and dumplings we had for dinner, I was back out in the woods. On the way down to my thinking place, I seen Mr. Weaver and Rex.

"Heidy, Mr. Weaver," I said.

"Heidy, girl," he said back.

I stopped to scratch old Rex behind the ears.

"How's your friend getting on?" Mr. Weaver asked.

I knowed he was talking about Be More. "He's okay, I reckon."

Then Mr. Weaver started to walk on off like he already forgot I was there.

"See you, Mr. Weaver," I hollered to him.

"See you, girl," he wheezed. He was shaking his head from side to side like he didn't believe something.

When I got down to my thinking place, I was surprised to see Bobby there.

"Hi, Annie," he said. "I figured you'd be coming down here sometime."

"How'd you know about this spot?" I asked, and I reckon I sounded a little bit insulted.

"I seen you here lots of times." Then he looked embarrassed, like he got caught with his finger in the pie. "I mean, heck, it ain't so far from my house no ways."

He was blushing for some reason. I figured I better say something fast before I started it, too. I don't like to blush.

"Pretty down here, ain't it?" I said.

"Annie," he said, getting right down to why he come, "do you think I could help out on the set design for that Thanksgiving Program?" He was looking down at the ground, kicking leaves around. "I didn't want to be no Pilgrim, and that crazy Zola Ann bothers me to no end."

"She's pretty, ain't she?" I sighed.

"She's crazy! She's always follering me around and batting her eyelashes at me," he said. "Anyhow, I like drawing and fixing things up. Reckon I could help out any?"

We made a pact right then and there that he would help me get things ready for the program, and I would help keep Zola Ann away from him. That wouldn't be a easy thing to do, but it was something I wouldn't mind trying.

I was a crystal again!

Chapter 15

My set designing work was going real good, but it had to be put off for a week. It was Halloween, and we was all busy getting ready. At school we was decorating our class and making little favors to take over to Children's Hospital. At home we was making big plans.

We celebrated lots of holidays out at our place, but I reckon Halloween was the most fun. Christmas was fun, too, but we never talked about Christmas for months after it was gone, and we didn't sit and talk about all the Christmases gone by while we was readying for that year's. So, I reckon Halloween come in first when you got right down to it.

That year Halloween come on Friday, so all the kids come over to our house on Thursday night to make our plans. Junior drawed out a map of the whole neighborhood and spread it out on the front room floor. First thing he pointed to, and I knowed it would be, was the secret graveyard.

I reckon I have to tell you about that, even if I don't like it none. Fact is, Junior always thought hisself to be like Tom Sawyer, and Charles Edward to be like Huck Finn. They was a lot like them, but sometimes they carried it a little too far. Junior's favorite part in Tom Sawyer was when Tom and Huck was out in the woods burying that old dead cat. That's where he got the idea that we should bury a cat every Halloween.

The graveyard was way on out past Granny's house, up the hill, and under a old dead tree that was growed all around with briars. This year there would be seven little graves up there. I didn't like that part of Halloween night. It scared the pants off me, but if I wanted to go along with everything else, I had to go with that, too.

Last year was the first time Danny went up there with us. Lou usually kept her hands over her eyes the whole time, but last year it took all the hands we both had just to keep Danny from running off through the woods.

Junior looked around to make sure Mama or Daddy wasn't in the room, and then asked, "Freddy Wayne, you got the cat?"

Freddy Wayne and Jimmy both started laughing like crazy. Finally, Freddy Wayne managed to say, "Yeah, I got the cat." And they both cracked up again.

"You want to tell us about it?" Junior asked. There was rules about getting the cat. Mainly that it couldn't be just a found dead cat. We all knowed better than to touch something dead like that. It had to be a growed up cat that had been run over or something.

"It's okay," Freddy Wayne said, soon as he quit laughing. "It was one of Mrs. Bybee's cats what got run over out on Hayes Street last summer." He grinned real big, and looked to make sure everyone was listening before he went on. "I put it in a shoe box, wrapped it up good, and stuck it in the freezer."

Freddy Wayne didn't say many things that I thought was funny, but even I laughed at that. I could just see Aunt Virginia pulling that cat out of the freezer to thaw for supper. She'd be ten counties away before anyone ever found out what happened.

When the laughing died down so as he could be heard, Junior said, "Let's get on with it. Anybody got any ideas for tricks?"

"How about the Indian's grave?" Danny asked. "We could dig it up."

That brought complete silence to the room. It was funny. Danny was scared of his shadow, but he was probably the only one of all us kids that weren't scared silly of that Indian's grave. And do you think for one minute Junior, Freddy Wayne, or one of them big boys was gonna admit to little Danny that they was just plain scared of that place?

"Ain't no full moon," Junior said real quick-like, and I recalled that just last night it was as close to full as it ever was gonna get without being full. Thank goodness Danny didn't pay no attention to the moon, or he would of been all-too-glad to argue the point.

"Whose door we gonna get this year?" Billy asked.

We all laughed remembering a few years back when we took Old Man Fox's outhouse door with him sitting inside, taking care of business. Every year we took the door off somebody's outhouse and throwed it in the creek. But it weren't never the same after Old Man Fox's.

"How about Uncle Frank and Aunt Virginia this year?" Junior asked, and everybody agreed. "Swear you won't say nothing," he said to Freddy Wayne and Jimmy.

"Not a word," they both said, and held up their hands like to swear.

"Don't forget we got to soap Doc Elder's windows," Jerry said.

"That's right!" Charles Edward interrupted. "Else we won't get a ice cream cone for cleaning all the soap off on Saturday."

We was all looking at the map, trying to think of another good trick. Be More Happy's place stood out like a sore thumb. That's usually where most of the tricks was played. Nobody said nothing, but I could tell they was disappointed that he weren't quite as spooky as he use to be. And Freddy Wayne kept looking over at me and curling up his lip in a sneer.

Then it was, Bobby hollered, "Yeow!" And jumped clean off the floor. "I got it! I got it!" he said over and over, clapping them boys on the back.

"Sit down, Bobby, before you have a fit," Junior said. "Tell us what it is you got."

"We can wash Old Man Fox's truck!" His eyes was shining with excitement, but everybody else just sat there dumb-like. Then, one by one, grins started spreading over everybody's faces when they caught on to what he meant.

Bobby went ahead and explained. "Remember last summer? Me and Junior and Charles Edward wanted to wash that nasty old thing, and he wouldn't let us."

"Swore it didn't need washing," Charles Edward put in.

"All the while, it sat there drawing more flies than a dead horse," Junior said, and everybody laughed.

"That's a good one," Freddy Wayne said, looking at Bobby. "I didn't know you had it in you."

Bobby blushed, and I wanted to kick Freddy Wayne. You might know, if he ever did say anything good to a person, he'd have to cover it over with something bad.

Mama called us to the kitchen for hot chocolate then, and while we was sitting at the table, we decided who would bring the soap, brushes, and stuff for washing that old truck. Daddy heard what we was planning and offered to let us use his car wax. He looked like he'd like to go along and help out.

The next day was one of the longest I ever lived, but nighttime finally did come. We was too excited to eat. I reckon Mama knowed it, 'cause all she fixed for supper was chili, and we didn't even eat all that.

Soon as we was finished eating, we went and got into our costumes. I was a witch. I wore a old black dress of Mama's that come all the way to the floor, a witch's hat, and a mask. I reckon I looked as scary as most. Danny was a ghost. He wore a piece of a old sheet, a ghost mask, and Mama powdered his hair with flour. And Lou was a pirate lady. She didn't look scary at all, but I reckon that's the way she wanted it.

Bobby and Billy and Jerry stopped by our house on the way over to Aunt Dorothy's. She was gonna take us all up to Hillcrest to trick-or-treat a few houses. They weren't but nine houses out around us. That weren't enough to even start to fill a trick-or-treat bag. When we was done up at Hillcrest, we come back out to our place for the most fun.

First off, we trick-or-treated the houses in our neighborhood. They was the best, 'cause everybody knowed everybody, and they all give out good stuff like cupcakes and cookies. Soon as we was finished trick-or-treating, it was time to go up to the secret graveyard and bury the cat.

We stopped by Freddy Wayne's house on the way up to pick up the cat, and from the smell of things, he must of took it out of the freezer too soon.

I ain't gonna tell you what it was like, burying that cat. You want to know, you go bury one your own self. All I'm gonna say is, I was sure glad to have it over and done with. Just like last year, me and Lou had to hold on tight to Danny. Sometimes I wondered if that boy was ever gonna grow up. But what happened later that night made up my mind for sure about that.

When we finished up at the graveyard, we walked on down to Doc Elder's place and soaped his windows real good. Next thing, we went back out to Freddy Wayne's house, took the door off their outhouse, and threw it in the creek. It was really getting spooky by then. Black clouds hid the moon so good it was pitch dark except for when, ever so often, lightning would flash across the sky. Then thunder would rumble off in the distance, and I started wishing real hard that we was home, safe and sound.

Before we could go home, though, we still had to wash and wax Old Man Fox's truck. We stopped by my house and got the scrub brush and bucket. Daddy made certain we didn't forget the wax. Then we was off to do our last trick.

On the way down to Old Man Fox's house, Billy and Jerry was fussing about not getting to go to Be More Happy's place. I told them boys that I knowed it weren't 'cause of me they weren't going down there. When did they ever do me any favors? They was just plain scared! I reckon that's when they decided that if they didn't want to make themselves out to be a bunch of scaredy cats, they was gonna have to go on down there to trick-or-treat, anyway. And that's what we did. Soon as we walked into the clearing where his house was, Freddy Wayne grabbed me and pushed me up to the front of the group.

"Since you ain't scared of that old spook, you lead the way," he said.

Inside, I felt like I wouldn't never be sure about Be More. Too many strange things was always happening. But I'd croak before I'd let on to them boys. So, shaking on the inside, but acting brave on the outside, I walked on up to the back door and knocked real loud. The kitchen light switched on, and Be More opened up the door.

"Trick-or-treat!" I hollered all by myself, and I had to look back to make sure everybody hadn't left. They was there. Cringing in the shadows.

Even out there on that dark back porch, I could see Be More's eyes light up. He was glad we come. He didn't say nothing. He never did talk much when anybody was around. Holding up a finger to signal us to wait, he disappeared into the house, and come back a minute later with a big basket of bananas, oranges, and apples, and let us have our pick. Them boys sure come out of the shadows for that.

When we left Be More's, I felt great. I was glad we went, but now that it was all over, them boys seemed to be right disappointed that he hadn't jumped out of the bushes and started chopping off heads or something.

Another streak of lightning hurried us on over to Old Man Fox's place. We had to use branch water to wash with, 'cause he was still up and we didn't want him to hear the water running. Washing that truck weren't no easy thing to do. I don't reckon it'd ever been washed before. Some of the boys scrubbed with the brushes, and soon as they got a place clean, the others would run down to the branch and get more water to rinse with. Then me and Lou would dry off the clean place. It must of took us a hour to get that truck cleaned and waxed. It was getting pretty late by the time we headed home.

Washing that truck was the last of our tricks, and I was glad of it. We crossed over the creek and headed on up Garvin street with our mouths all stuffed full of candy. Then it was I discovered they was a lot more to my little brother than I ever knowed about. Just when we was passing by the Indian's grave, a streak of lightning lit up the sky, and this terrible looking white thing come up off the ground right on top of the grave and started jumping around and hollering something awful. For a minute we all froze stiff, then them boys took off running like the devil was after them. It didn't take but just a minute for me and Lou to figure out that it was Danny, but if them boys ever found out, they'd never let him stop paying for it. It was hard to keep from laughing right out, but we didn't let on.

The next morning we was up bright and early. Nobody wanted to miss seeing Old Man Fox's face when he seen his truck. Me and Lou and Danny all got down to his place and hid in the bushes and waited. Them boys was already there when we got there. They must of started out early and went the long way around. It was for sure they didn't come by our house. The path what led to Old Man Fox's from our house passed right by the Indian's grave. That could of had something to do with it.

Sitting out there in the bright sunshine, that old truck fairly glistened. Soon as that old man stuck his head out the door, he seen what had happened. He walked all around his shiny old truck, scratching his head. Then he kicked the tire a couple of times, said some words I ain't allowed to say, jumped in, and roared off down the road, trying to raise as much dirt as possible.

We all laughed till our sides hurt, and Junior said, "That old man will probably spit hisself to death trying to dirty up that truck today."

Remembering back on it, it's hard to say which was the best trick, Old Man Fox's truck or what Danny done to them boys. But when you come right down to it, I reckon they ain't nothing puts a smile on my face like seeing them boys running off through the woods half scared to death.

Chapter 16

Halloween was over, but I won't never forget what Danny done. If I live to be a hundred, I won't never figure out where he got the courage to lay down right on top of that Indian's grave. They weren't no figuring that boy.

My set designing job come off real good. I reckon I ought to say our set designing job, 'cause Bobby done ever' bit as much work on it as I did, even if he didn't get none of the credit for it.

The whole program come off good. Danny stumbled and fell down three times when he was dragging that heavy velvet curtain acrost the stage, but everybody laughed like it was cute. Lou's song was perfect, and I was as proud as if I was standing up there singing myself. I didn't even mind Zola Ann looking at Bobby like she owned him. I knowed better. Didn't nobody own Bobby! And them boys all made good Indians. They was always wild, and being dressed up like Indians, they looked like they was right in place.

Anyhow, that was over and done with, and I was glad of it. We had one more day of school and then—Thanksgiving vacation. Four whole days of no school. And we was having company.

Lou asked Mama a long time ago if Mildred could spend the holiday with us. Her mother and daddy was in Colorado and they left Mildred behind with the housekeeper. I don't reckon I know why they would go off and leave Mildred behind, but I figured that was their business. People does strange things sometimes.

Mama come to get us after school and we went on up to Hillcrest to get some things at the store. The smell of celery and oranges in the store made me hungry for Thanksgiving dinner. Mama got the sugar and cranberry sauce she come for, and then we stood in a line about a mile-and-a-half long while everybody else that had forgot something got checked out.

After the grocery store, we went to pick up Mildred at her house. I never thought I'd know someone that lived in a house like that. This must be the "rich" Freddy Wayne was always talking about. It was a huge house made all out of rocks and looked like it belonged in one of them fairytale books. Mildred come out to the car dressed in blue jeans and a old blue jean jacket. She didn't look like somebody that lived in a big house like that, she looked just like everybody else. I always thought rich people was supposed to be different.

When we got home, I stayed around the house just long enough to be polite to Mildred, and then I headed on out in the woods for a while. Most all the leaves already fell from the trees, and they looked cold and empty. It weren't really cold yet, just real brisk, and on that day, they weren't one corner in them woods what didn't smell like pumpkin pies or something good baking for someone's Thanksgiving dinner. I walked on up, all the way to the top of the "H" Street hill. Weren't nobody else out. The woods was always lonely in the winter. I was hoping to see Be More Happy, but he weren't out, either. I hadn't seen him since I stopped by his place to tell him about Halloween night.

I can't exactly explain how it was I felt right then. I was glad it was Thanksgiving, glad about the turkey Mama had out thawing at home, but inside I was sorry. I was sorry for all the people that didn't have the sweet smell of pumpkin pie baking in their kitchens. I was feeling bad about Be More being all alone and not having a Thanksgiving dinner or no one to share it with. But it was more than that, more like I was sorry that the whole world weren't as lucky as I was.

Going back down the hill, I seen Mr. Weaver and Rex out walking. He was wearing that old tore up sweater of his. Aunt Virginia knitted him a new one last year for Christmas, but he never wore it, said it was too nice, and he'd only get it dirty. Rex come running up to meet me when I got down to where they was.

"Heidy, Mr. Weaver," I said.

"Heidy, girl," he answered. "Who's the company?"

Beats me how Mr. Weaver always knowed what was going on thereabouts. If you ask me, he was the spooky one. I reckon if it weren't for him being Freddy Wayne and Jimmy's granddaddy, them boys would of been making up tales about him, too.

"One of Lou's friends from school," I said, answering his question. "Her mama and daddy is gone somewhere, so she's spending Thanksgiving with us. How'd you know we had company?"

He laughed that wheezy laugh. "Old Rex knowed it," he said, patting his dog on the head. "Reckon old Rex knows everything."

Before I could ask more questions, he was walking on up the hill with old Rex close behind. I reckon that old man puzzled me ever' bit as much as Be More.

I went on back home to help Mama with supper. It being the night before Thanksgiving, we wouldn't be having much, but I'd be expected to help anyway. Lou and Mildred was in the kitchen when I got home. We was having soup and sandwiches for supper and Lou was trying to show Mildred how to use a can opener. I don't reckon I ever knowed anyone what couldn't even open a can.

"Don't you ever help out in the kitchen?" I asked, and got a very mean look from Lou.

Mildred smiled. "No, I'm not allowed. Mama says that's Mrs. Green's job, and I shouldn't bother her.

"You mean you never made cookies or nothing?" I asked even though Lou was still giving me the evil eye.

Mildred shook her head no, and Lou said, "Annie, some people have more to do than to spend all their time in the kitchen."

They both left the kitchen then. I couldn't help but to feel sorry for Mildred. Making cookies and helping in the kitchen was fun.

"Annie," Mama said, "did you hear me?"

"I'm sorry, Mama," I answered. "I was thinking. What did you say?"

"Mr. Weaver brought by a hen a little while ago," she repeated.

So that's how he knew we had company!

"Said he already killed it when Aunt Virginia come by to ask him to go over and eat with them." She stopped to take a hot bubbly mincemeat pie out of the oven. "So, I was thinking, maybe we could put it in the oven with the turkey tomorrow, and fix up a little of everything else for you to take down to Be More Happy."

Why didn't I think of that? All I thought of was Be More not having a good Thanksgiving, but nothing to change it. Mama was nice. She was always thinking up ways to help other people.

After that, I talked Mama's ear off about what to take, how to fix it, how to carry it down to his place, and a million other things.

When supper was over we watched a program on television, then me and Lou and Mildred went to our room. Lou and Mildred played checkers while I talked. I reckon Lou was right to keep giving me them dirty looks, 'cause most of my talking was questions I didn't have no right to ask. Mildred didn't seem to mind, though. She was real friendly.

It weren't easy to get to sleep that night what with Lou and Mildred giggling, and all the thinking I was doing about Be More's dinner. But even with not sleeping, I was the first one up the next morning. First kid,

I mean. Mama was always the last one to go to bed and the first one up. Sometimes I wondered if she ever did sleep.

"Morning, Annie," Mama said. She was just getting the turkey out of the icebox.

"Morning, Mama," I said and yawned.

"Them girls keep you awake all night, too?" she asked while she was buttering two big slices of nut bread to put under the broiler. Thanksgiving and Christmas was the only two days of the year we didn't have to eat a egg for breakfast. I reckon Mama figured we'd be getting enough to eat, it wouldn't matter if we missed one little egg.

Me and Mama ate our breakfast of nut bread and hot chocolate together. The rest of the morning was spent making the stuffing, baking the turkey, cutting up fruit for fruit salad, and fixing something to eat for the rest of the people that come wandering into the kitchen at all hours.

At ten o'clock, Be More's hen was ready to come out of the oven. It was perfect, a beautiful golden brown, and plump with Mama's stuffing which was the best to be had anywhere. I cut a big slice of pumpkin pie, and then decided maybe he'd like mincemeat, too. Lou and Mildred fixed up a little bowl of fruit salad to go with everything. The only thing slowing us down was the gravy. That come last. Mama says gravy ain't good unless it's fresh made. While she was making that, she put a couple of rolls in the oven to brown.

Finally, it was all ready and spread out on the kitchen table. The gravy was in a mason jar. There was another jar filled with succotash, a little dish of cranberry sauce, the bowl of fruit salad, rolls, the pie, and of course the hen. It all looked and smelled delicious. We helped Mama to pack it all into her laundry basket, and me and Danny carried it down to Be More's place.

I couldn't believe how cold it turned overnight. The leaves was rattling around on the ground like old bones. I was starting to worry that the food in the basket was gonna freeze before we made it down to Be More's. When we got down there, the place looked deserted. His truck weren't nowhere to be seen, even the chickens was quiet. I knocked on the door, and for a while, it seemed like he weren't gonna be home.

"I reckon we should of told him what we was gonna do," I said to Danny.

"I wish you had," he come back. "That basket ain't light you know, and my fingers is froze blue!"

Just when he got those words out, Be More opened the door.

"Annie! Danny!" he said. "Come on in here before you freeze to death."

Picking up the basket, we stepped inside on the small closed part of the back porch. "We brung you something, Be More," I said through my chattering teeth.

"Whatever it is, it sure does smell good," he said. Then he opened up the door to his house, and said, "You two come on inside. I'll make you some tea to warm you up a little."

I couldn't figure how tea was gonna warm us up. But I didn't give it a whole lot of thought. I was too busy noticing what we had just come into. I never in my life seen nothing like it. Me and Danny just stood there with our mouths hanging open. Be More's house was beautiful on the inside. It looked like those houses in the magazines. The ones that you don't reckon real people live in.

Be More interrupted my thinking. "There, that will be ready in just a minute," he said walking away from the stove. "What's in the basket, Annie?"

Then I told him all about how we come to have the extra hen, and Mama thinking about him. He was real pleased that we thought of him, and he made a big fuss about how delicious everything looked and smelled while I took it all out of the basket and loaded it on his cabinet top.

While I was doing that, there was a loud whistling sound from the stove that almost caused me to drop the cranberry sauce into the fruit salad. Come to find out it was the tea kettle. We was gonna have *hot* tea.

Me and Danny sat quietly and sipped the hot tea. We ain't never had it before, but it weren't as bad as I thought it would be. Of course, Danny kept giving me looks like he thought Be More was trying to poison us.

From where I was sitting, I could see into the front room. It was beautiful, too. All the furniture was old, but it looked like new. The parts of the house that I could see was real light and brightly colored. I never would of thought it would be like that. Not seeing it from the outside!

We talked about a lot of things, like how cold it was, and if maybe it would snow, but Be More never said nothing about his house. I know he took note of how surprised we was, but he never said nothing.

Before we left, we thanked him for the tea, and he thanked us for the dinner we brung. Then we was back out in them cold woods. I was wanting to think on what I just saw, but Danny, who hadn't said a word the whole time we was at Be More's, wouldn't stop talking for a minute. He talked the whole way home and didn't even stop to take a breath when we got in the house. Before I got a chance to say anything, he told all about it.

Mama looked to me. "Is that true, Annie?"

"I reckon it is," I answered. "You have to see it, Mama. It's just like in the magazines." There was a long, thoughtful silence, and then I said, "Be

More didn't even say nothing about it. Like everybody lived in a house like that."

Mildred come in just then, so we dropped the subject and started off talking about how cold it was getting.

"My ears is so cold, I can't even feel them no more," I said.

"What you need is a hat," Mildred said, and she got up and left the kitchen real sudden-like. When she come back, I was setting the table.

"Annie, do you think your Mama would let you have this?" She held out a beautiful white furry hat.

Mama did let me have it. Mildred explained that she had a whole lot of hats at home, but no little sister, and that if she could have a little sister, she'd want one just like me.

Thanksgiving dinner was delicious like it always was. I reckon it was because of what we done for Be More that I didn't feel guilty no more about what I had. They was all kinds of other feelings going around inside me though. It was strange, but I felt sorry for Mildred. A person would of thought she'd have anything she wanted, but she didn't. So I reckon it was like Be More said, money ain't what makes a person rich or happy. And I reckon he ought to know. He was one of the saddest people I ever knowed, and from the looks of things, money weren't his problem. Weren't even close to it!

Chapter 17

What I seen on Thanksgiving Day worried me to no end. Maybe it wouldn't of been so bad if Danny hadn't seen it, too, but he kept on insisting that he knowed all about Be More Happy now.

"Ain't no secret no more," he said more than once. "That old man's a robber."

"How can you say things like that when he's been so nice to all of us?" I asked him, trying to reason, but it appeared he had his mind set.

"That's just his cover-up," he said, like he knowed everything. "He's just nice as long as he thinks we're stupid." Then Danny's eyes got real big. He scared hisself again. "Soon as he thinks we caught on to what he's doing, he'll probably be coming after us."

Right then was when I made a really bad mistake. I could of scared Danny half to death, and made sure he never said nothing to no one about what he seen at Be More's house. But I didn't. I didn't like scaring people. I reckon I should of done it, though, 'cause he went right out and told them boys all about what he seen, and they come to the same conclusion he did.

It was later on, that same afternoon, I had cause to regret not scaring the pants off that little brat when I had the chance. I was way up at the top of the "H" Street hill, back in the woods a way, picking up pecans for Mama, when I heard a car coming. I looked up, and seeing it was Be More, I run out to the road. But by the time I got there, he was already passed.

Then it was, I seen them boys scrambling around down at the bottom of the hill, hiding behind trees, rocks, bushes, whatever they could get behind. Just when Be More's truck come around the curve and down a little, they started pelting it with rocks. I reckon it scared Be More pretty bad, 'cause he stopped for a minute like he didn't know what was happening. Then he started up and roared on off down the road.

I headed on down the hill, running just as fast as I could. Reckon I was mad enough to tackle a grizzly bear, or even Freddy Wayne and all them boys put together. By the time I got down to where they was, they was all rolling around on the ground laughing. It weren't all of them, though, just Charles Edward, Freddy Wayne, Jimmy, Billy, and Jerry.

"Real funny!" I hollered at them, and they all got real quiet.

"Well, lookie who's here with us," Freddy Wayne sneered.

"I ain't *with* you!" I was still hollering. "I just come down here to tell you that I seen what you done, and I'm telling this time! I'm telling your mamas!"

Charles Edward's face turned white, and he started to say something, but Freddy Wayne interrupted him. "You ain't telling nothing," he said, and pushed me backward. "Know why we hid, Miss Smart Mouth?" He pushed me back again. "We hid so that old man wouldn't know who *wasn't* throwing rocks at him." He pushed me again. "You don't know no better than to associate with crooks, so we're gonna help you out a little, and make it so crooks won't have nothing to do with you." Then he pushed me again, but this time I kicked him hard, right on his leg.

Freddy Wayne don't take kindly to being kicked. His face turned red, his eyes bugged out, and he was just about to push me again when the most gosh-awful sound I ever heard come from a little ways up the hill. It was a terrible moaning and rustling around in the bushes. All them boys just stood there staring off in the direction that noise come from. Then it come again, and they lit out of there like a bat out of Utah!

Ever since Halloween, them boys has been careful about going out in the woods alone, or even together, if it was close to getting dark. I reckon they thought that Indian was after them for sure. Call it stupid if you want to, but far as I know, they weren't nothing in them woods to be scared of, so I stuck around to see what it was making that terrible noise.

Sure enough, soon as them boys was out of sight, Bobby come walking out of the bushes. "That Freddy Wayne is the biggest bully I ever seen," he said. "I never knowed no boy what would pick on a girl the way he does."

"He ain't as mean as he acts," I said. "But some days he's just real good at acting."

Then we both laughed till our sides hurt. Mama was always saying that the one who laughs last, laughs best. I reckon that was the day I finally figured out what she meant by that.

"Did you see what they done?" I asked Bobby.

"All I seen was Freddy Wayne pushing you around," he said.

Then I told him what they did to Be More, and how they hid so he wouldn't know who his friends was.

"How come them to start that up again?" he asked. "I thought we was at peace with the old man."

"I reckon Danny told them about Be More's house," I explained. "We went down there on Thanksgiving to take him some stuff Mama fixed for him, and he asked us to come in. You wouldn't believe it, Bobby. The place is like a mansion on the inside. It was beautiful! Anyhow, Danny said he knowed how come him to have a house like that. He says Be More is a robber."

Bobby thought for a long while, then he asked, "What do you think, Annie?"

"I don't think I know how he come by such a beautiful house," I answered. "But I know Be More, and I don't think he'd do nothing dishonest."

Bobby thought again, and finally he said, "Well, I reckon you know him better than anyone else around here, so if you say he's okay, he's okay!"

We grinned at each other. Then Bobby pulled his pocketknife out of his pocket, and looked in my eyes, but he weren't grinning no more. He come over to where I was sitting on a rock, and I held out my hand. I knowed what he wanted. He opened up his knife and cut a slash across my thumb and then his own. Then we held them together and let our blood mix. We was friends for life.

It was a long time before either one of us said anything. I reckon we was both embarrassed. Finally, I said, "I reckon I better get back up the hill and get Mama's pecans. I left them up there when I seen what was happening."

Bobby walked up the hill with me. We talked about a lot of things that didn't mean much, but I liked being with Bobby. He weren't at all like them other boys.

After we come back down the hill, and Bobby went on to his house, I got to thinking about what happened with them boys a little while ago. Then it was I decided to find out once and for all about Be More Happy! And I knowed who would be able to answer all my questions.

Doc Elder's place was warm and cozy on the inside, and smelled like boxed candy and wrapping paper. The windows was all frosted over, making it look like Christmas, and sure enough, Doc Elder was getting out his Christmas decorations when I come in. I put my dime down on the counter and asked for a cup of hot chocolate.

My worries must of showed on my face, 'cause soon as Doc Elder set the cup in front of me, he said, "What's troubling you today, Annie?"

"Lots of things, Doc Elder," I answered, but I waited a while before I went on. "Have you ever been inside Be More Happy's house?"

"No, I haven't," he answered, and looked at me with one eyebrow raised up high. "Why do you ask?"

I told him all about what had happened on Thanksgiving and how Be More never said a word about it and all. He didn't look surprised to hear it, either. Then I told him what just happened with them boys, and what they was saying about Be More.

"I reckon I just have to find out what the truth is," I said, trying hard not to cry. Then I explained why I come to him. "I can't ask Be More. Seems like I'm always saying things that make him sad, and anyhow, I figured you'd know about him."

Doc Elder had a faraway look in his eyes. He put down what he was doing and come and sat down next to me, sighing like he was giving up some big fight. "You really like that old man, huh, Annie?"

"He's my friend, Doc Elder. At first, I was just as scared of him as them boys are, but I looked in his eyes." I stopped to think for a minute and then went on. "His eyes was so lonely it made me want to cry. But now, most times, they twinkle."

"And you made them twinkle, Annie, you know that?" he said.

"I didn't do nothing," I said. "Fact is, he's the one does for me. He always knows just what to say to make me feel good about things."

"That's the way it is with friends, Annie. They give to each other without ever knowing it." He smiled at me, but his smile went away when he said, "It's too bad Be More didn't have a friend like you when he needed it most."

"What do you mean by that, Doc Elder?" I asked, and sipped my hot chocolate.

He looked at me long and hard before he answered. "Annie, I'm going to tell you something I've never told anyone. And I want you to understand that the only reason I'm telling you is because you are Be More's friend, and I know you'll not be using it against him."

My hands was sweating. That was what I been waiting on, to hear about Be More, but right about then, I weren't too sure I wanted to know.

Doc Elder took a deep breath and then started his story. "It all started about forty years ago. There was a brilliant young man by the name of Harold Jenkins. He was thirty-four years old and already running for governor of the state. I had just graduated from college and was busy trying to get started out as a pharmacist, and helping my daddy with the store, but I still remember how Jenkins was idolized by all the young people. He was young, handsome, athletic, and most of all, he had dreams for the future, and he shared those dreams with the whole state.

"His wife was one of the most beautiful women I've ever seen. Not just in looks, either. She had a sweetness about her that made everybody that ever met her feel like they were really somebody special. And that little girl! She was a carbon copy of her mother. Everywhere Jenkins went, he took them along. I never saw a man prouder of his family.

"Then one night, right in the middle of his campaign, a terrible thing happened. He and his wife and little daughter had been to a big campaign dinner up in the northwest part of the state. During dinner, he got a message that his daddy was in the hospital back down here with a heart attack. He was determined to get back home, and headed out in spite of several people warning him about the fog that had rolled in over the hills. Well, as fate would have it, he didn't make it to see his daddy that night. There was a terrible accident. His wife and daughter were both killed, and to top it all off, his daddy died later on that same night.

"Jenkins was really in a bad way, and I don't suppose it helped any when the newspaper came out the next morning calling him a cocky young politician who couldn't take a warning, who wasn't capable of making a wise decision. They as much as said he had murdered his wife and daughter.

"Then it was like he dropped off the face of the earth. His campaign manager withdrew Jenkins's name from the campaign. No one heard another word from Harold Jenkins until that day, ten years later, when he walked right through that door.

"He looked like he had aged a hundred years. The only reason I knew who he was was because of the house. I kept the keys for it, like my daddy did before me. They always left them here in case of an emergency, and then they would stop by to get them when they came out. This was way out in the country in those days, and they used that house as a kind of retreat. A place to get away from the city, and let down their hair for a while.

"I remember that day well. Mr. Weaver was sitting over there at that table resting his feet when the front door opened, and this wild-looking creature come in, walked up to the counter right over there, and asked for the keys to the creek house. He and his daddy were the only ones that ever called it that. So anyway, I gave him the keys, and he looked at me with those cold black eyes like he was begging me not to say anything.

"Mr. Weaver and I decided right then that if he wanted people to know his business, it was up to him. And from what we have seen over the last thirty years, his privacy is what he seems to treasure most. That was the reason he ran away from the sheriff that day by the creek. Can you imagine what the newspapers would have done if they had found out that Harold Jenkins had been right under their noses all these years?"

Doc Elder didn't say nothing else. He started wiping off the countertop. When I felt him looking at me, I said, "Thanks, Doc Elder, I figured it would be something like that." Then I jumped down off my stool, and said, "I reckon I better be getting on home."

Doc Elder was watching me like I was a stick of dynamite that was set to go off any minute. "You okay, Annie?" he asked.

I told him I was okay, I just had a lot to think about, and he give me a licorice stick to eat on the way home. I don't remember walking home. I don't even remember the cold. I was too busy thinking. Everything was fitting together. All the crazy things Mr. Weaver had said that day down by the creek weren't so crazy after all. Be More talking about dying inside. Now I knowed why he felt that way. His house. Everything made sense at last. But I weren't too sure I was glad about it. I knowed all along he weren't crooked. But now! Now I'd have to do something for sure, to see that Be More didn't get hurt no more.

I got home and everything was the same. I won't never understand how it is, that someone's whole life can change and nobody even notices it. Mama was in the kitchen getting supper started, Danny was playing with his cars on the floor, and Lou was practicing her piano lesson. Daddy would be home pretty soon, but he wouldn't know, either. The most that would happen would be that someone would say, "What you so quiet about, Annie?" But I wouldn't say. I'd just shrug and wouldn't tell nobody nothing. For a minute there, I had the feeling that I knowed how Be More Happy must feel all the time. Sad and alone.

Chapter 18

I stayed around the house for the most part of the next week, thinking about what Doc Elder told me. It didn't take me long to figure out that being sad about something what happened so long ago weren't gonna do no one no good, and I had other things to do. It was December. Christmas would be coming soon enough, and I needed to be out in the woods gathering things up. I figured as long as I was out anyway, I might as well go on down to Be More's place. I hadn't seen him in a while.

Dragging a bag along for pinecones, berries, and pine boughs, I headed on out to the woods. It was cold as blue blazes! But the woods was beautiful. The grass and leaves made a crisp crunching sound every step along the way, and before I knowed it, I was at Be More's house. He was outside filling up his bird feeders.

"Hello, Annie," he said when he seen me coming up.

"Hi, Be More," I answered back.

"What brings you out on such a cold day?" he asked while he was putting the lid on the last bird feeder.

I held up my bag and said, "Looking for pinecones and berries for Christmas decorations."

He squinted like he was thinking on something real hard, then he said, "I know where there's some mistletoe. If you can stand the company of an old man, I might help out. Might even know where there's a bird's nest."

"What do you want with a bird's nest?" I asked, truly puzzled.

"You don't know that a bird's nest in your Christmas tree will bring you good luck?"

I laughed. I never heard that one before, but I reckon Be More knowed what he was talking about. He seemed to be smarter than most.

Be More went inside his house, put on a hat, and was back out in a flash. He looked funny with his long white hair hanging out from under the flaps he had turned down over his ears. He brought out one of his hats for me to wear, and it was more than a little bit too big. I reckon I looked funny, too.

"Don't you have a hat, Annie?" he asked when he put it on my head.

I answered, "Mildred give me one at Thanksgiving, but I don't wear it unless Mama makes me. It's made out of rabbit fur, and makes me feel bad for the poor little rabbit that had to give up his skin to keep my head warm.

Be More laughed, and we headed on out into the woods. Mostly, we was quiet. I had something on my mind that I wanted to say to Be More, and I reckon he was just enjoying the woods. They was so pretty in the winter! I reckon they weren't no time of the year that the woods weren't pretty. By the time we got to the top of the hill where the spring was, my bag was almost full of pinecones. Be More pointed high up in a old oak tree, and sure enough, there was a big bunch of mistletoe. While he was chucking rocks and sticks at the mistletoe to knock it out of the tree, I gathered up some pretty red berries from the bushes nearby.

I didn't notice before, but from where we was, you could look right down the hill to the place where them boys had been throwing rocks at Be More last week. I was standing there, looking down on that and remembering, when Be More come over and handed me a big bunch of mistletoe.

"Thanks, Be More," I said, and I seen he was looking down the hill, too. I figured that was as good a time as any to say what I had to say. "I seen them boys throwing rocks at you last week, Be More."

He just nodded and didn't say nothing, so I went on. "Be More, I have to tell you something. I won't never say nothing about it again, but since we're friends, I have to tell you." I looked into them eyes to see if he understood what I meant. It was like he knowed what I was gonna say before I said it. "I know, Be More. Doc Elder told me. He said he was telling me 'cause we was friends, and he thought maybe I could help you to be happy again."

When I looked back up at Be More, he was staring down the hill. I reckon he heard what I said, but he didn't say nothing. I was feeling real bad for hurting him again, but I was glad to have it said. Now I wouldn't never be accidentally saying things that was gonna make him feel bad.

After I stood there for a while, I got to figuring maybe he wanted to be alone, so I backed off and headed on down the hill. I weren't gone ten feet when a tall old man with white hair hanging out of his hat and twinkling black eyes said to me, "You're not going off without the bird's nest?"

I smiled, and tried hard to keep from jumping up and down. "I don't reckon. You know where one is?"

He led the way back down the hill, and when we was almost to his house, he slowed up and then pointed out some real heavy brush. Sure enough, there was a bird's nest. I went in after it and scratched the dickens out of myself doing it.

When we got back to Be More's house, I tried to divide up all the things we found, but he wouldn't have it. Said he didn't never decorate for Christmas. Not even a tree. I didn't argue with him. We said our goodbyes, and I left him his hat and went on home.

No Christmas tree? I'd see about that. Be More Happy was gonna have a merry Christmas if I had anything to do with it.

Things was really busy around home and at school. At home, we was already starting our baking and candy making. At school, we was doing a little bit of everything. There was a Christmas program, but it was just singing this time. We was making presents for our mamas and daddies, and all kinds of decorations for Christmas. Besides all that, I was making a neck scarf for Be More. Mama got some real pretty blue yarn and showed me how to do it, so now I hoped I just wouldn't make a mess of it.

On Saturday, Bobby come over to our house and we made presents for the birds. We smeared peanut butter all over some pinecones and then rolled them in birdseed. We was all having fun till Danny got a sprig of mistletoe out of the bag the pinecones was in and started hanging it over people's heads. I don't ordinarily get no thrill out of kissing. I been kissed all my life. But the kiss Bobby put on my cheek was like magic. It stayed there on my skin for the longest, and give me a warm, tingly feeling all over. I reckon it made him feel plenty warm, too, 'cause his face was as red as I ever seen it.

December fifteenth was what we called Christmas Tree Day, 'cause every year that's when we put up our tree. That year we got a special treat. To begin with, it was on a Saturday. But better than that, we woke up to find the whole place covered over with snow.

Breakfast, any time it snowed, was always thick steamy oatmeal with a big spoonful of brown sugar melting in the middle of it. As soon as that was down, warming our insides, we was out rolling in the snow. Thirty minutes later, we was all crowded around the stove trying to get warm, while Mama made up some hot chocolate. Later on, when everyone was dry and warm, Danny and Daddy took off in the car to go get a Christmas tree. I remembered then what I had to do that day.

Lou and Mama was sitting by the stove cracking pecans when I come into the kitchen all bundled up to go out again. I told Mama that I was going to find a Christmas tree for Be More Happy.

"Just make sure you don't cut down a tree that belongs to someone," she said.

"I won't, Mama," I answered, and started out the back door.

"Annie," Mama called out. "Put on your hat. I don't want a house full of sick kids for Christmas."

I went back to my room and put on the hat Mildred gave me. It was pretty enough, and as warm as any I ever had on my head, but I still felt bad for that poor little rabbit.

The woods looked like the winter wonderland we been singing about at school. I stopped and watched some little birds feeding on one of the pinecones we hung up last Saturday, then I headed on up the hill aways to get that tree. Not so far up the hill, I seen Mr. Weaver coming my way, carrying a gun under his arm.

"Heidy, girl," he said when he got down to where I was.

"Heidy, Mr. Weaver," I answered back. "You going hunting?"

"Reckon today's as good a day as any to get myself a rabbit or two," he said, and taking out a big handkerchief, blowed his nose. "Their tracks make it easy to find them in the snow."

Noticing the little pruning saw I was carrying, he asked, "Where you headed with that saw?"

"I gotta get a Christmas tree for Be More Happy," I said, glad he weren't talking about the rabbits anymore. He just stood there, looking at me real strange-like and nodding. Finally, he started to walk off, but stopped and said, "I'm gonna be back in behind Granny's for a spell. You stay clear. Don't want to be shooting no girl." He was still talking while he walked on off down the hill.

Mr. Weaver was always forgetting things. I wished he would forget that time. Forget he was hunting little rabbits.

When I was almost to the top of the Coolidge Street hill, I seen some little tracks in the snow and knowed right off they was rabbit tracks. I got to thinking about it all, and decided I wouldn't never be cold enough to need some poor little rabbit's skin to warm my head. Right then, I reached up and pulled that hat off my head and threw it into the bushes off to one side.

No sooner did that hat hit them bushes than I heard the firing of a rifle. Scared me so bad I let out a scream that scared the birds out of the trees. Then I heard feet running through the brush, and sure enough, there stood Freddy Wayne, his rifle barrel still smoking.

"Annie!" he said, looking from me to my hat down on the ground. "I thought ... are you okay?"

Now to be fair, I have to tell you here that Freddy Wayne may have been the brattiest person I ever knowed, but underneath all his meanness, he was good as gold. I never seen no one so sorry about anything.

"I'm okay," I said, and bent down to pick up my poor murdered hat. "You shot my hat!"

"I'll get you another one, Annie. I promise I will!" He looked like he was about to cry. Then he tried hard to straighten hisself up. "Don't you know better than to be fooling around in the woods when hunters is out?"

"Don't you know better than to shoot at something you ain't sure about?" I snapped back at him, and from the hurt look on his face, I was almost sorry I did.

"Annie, please. Don't say nothing to no one about this," he was almost begging. "I learned my lesson! Believe me. I'll be more careful from now on." He stopped to wipe the sweat off his face. Cold as it was, he was sweating. "You must of scared ten years off my life," he said.

I know I was being mean, but he needed to learn a lesson. Then it come to me, maybe he could learn two lessons! "You nearly took all the years off *my* life!" I shouted back at him, and then paused to make sure I had his attention. "I won't say nothing about this on one condition, Freddy Wayne."

"Anything, Annie. Anything you say." He sure was agreeable.

"You stop being so mean to Be More Happy, and see to it all the rest of them boys do it, too," I said, hoping I weren't pushing my luck too far.

"I knowed you was gonna say that," he said with his head ducked low. "I ain't got nothing against that old man, you either for that matter. I just get a kick out of teasing people." He looked at me close like to see if I was gonna believe that.

"Promise me you're gonna be nice?" I said.

"I promise, Annie. I promise on my life," he answered back.

I decided to make sure of that right then and there. "Good," I said. "I was just headed up the hill a ways to get a Christmas tree for his house. You can help."

He agreed to help me. We went on up the hill and cut the tree I had in mind. Freddy Wayne hefted it up on his shoulder, and we headed back down to Be More's house. On the way there, I remembered about the bird's nest. Freddy Wayne knowed where to get one, and while we was at it we got one for his house, too. I told him what Be More said about it bringing good luck.

We walked on down to Be More's, and I knocked on the door. "What's this we have here?" Be More said when he opened up the door.

"Me and Freddy Wayne brung you a Christmas tree, Be More," I said. "It ain't fitting not to have a tree in the house at Christmas." I was embarrassed.

After a while, Be More said, "I suppose you're right, Annie." Then he made a big fuss about the tree. "I see you even managed to find a bird's nest."

"Reckon you need luck just as much as the rest of us," I said.

Finally, Freddy Wayne spoke up. I was beginning to wonder what happened to his tongue. "If you have a hammer and some nails, I'll make up a stand for this real quick."

Be More showed him the tool shed, and while Freddy Wayne was hammering away in the shed, he come back out to me and said, "Annie Marcus, I don't suppose there is anything you can't do!"

I tried to look like I didn't know what he was talking about but couldn't. I just said, "I don't think Freddy Wayne will be giving you anymore trouble, Be More."

"I guess you're not going to tell me why?" he said with a big smile on his face.

I just shook my head no and laughed.

We wished Be More a Merry Christmas and left. Freddy Wayne said he was gonna walk me home to make sure I didn't get myself shot at. When we got to my house, I had him to wait while I run in and got him a big sprig of mistletoe.

"Thanks, Annie," he said with a gleam in his eye. I knowed what he'd be doing with that come Monday morning. "Thanks for everything," he said and looked like he meant it.

It seemed strange to me that even someone as mean as Freddy Wayne could be nice if he tried. But strange or not, I was glad. Freddy Wayne may have been the meanest kid I knowed, but he would drop dead in his tracks before he'd go back on his word.

We put up our tree that night, and after it was all decorated, Mama turned out all the lights in the house but those on the tree. We all sat around it drinking eggnog and talking about Christmas. I knew I could never talk about what happened that morning, but I'd always have the memory of it.

Chapter 19

The next couple of weeks Mama had everybody running errands for her. "Go get this! Stir that! Chop these!" Seems to me I spent most of my time out in the woods picking up pecans.

Funniest thing happened one afternoon. Me and Bobby had just about froze ourselves to death trying to find a few more pecans and was headed on home. Then we seen Old Man Fox coming through the woods. He was dancing a jig as he walked along and singing to hisself. It ain't normal to see that old man in the woods, and I don't recall ever seeing him so happy. Me and Bobby looked at each other like to say, "This is crazy," and without saying a word decided to follow him and see what he was up to.

We followed that old man on up the hill in the most crooked path you ever seen. Him giggling, singing, and clicking his heels together the whole way. I could of swore he was lost, but I reckon he weren't. Pretty soon he come to a spot where he stopped and put a finger up to his lips like to tell hisself to be quiet. Then I seen it. That crazy old man had his truck hid out in some bushes. I ain't exaggerating when I tell you it took him better than fifteen minutes to get that truck out of them bushes, and it not twenty feet to the road. I ain't never drove no car, but I reckon I could of done better than that.

Me and Bobby stepped out of the woods and watched while he drove on off down the hill weaving from one side of the road to the other. Mr. Weaver was there, too. He was resting on a stump across the road. Finally, when Old Man Fox was out of sight, Mr. Weaver said, "Heidy, girl. Heidy, boy." He was still looking after that old man like he could see further than me and Bobby.

"Heidy, Mr. Weaver," we both said together.

"You two see where he come from?" Mr. Weaver asked.

I answered, "We followed him through the woods." I stopped, and looked at Bobby like to tell him to tell the rest.

"He sure was acting strange. Singing. Dancing. Even had his old truck hid out in the bushes in there. What do you reckon is wrong with him?" Bobby sounded truly concerned. He was always concerned about everybody.

"Reckon he got a little too much Christmas cheer," Mr. Weaver said. "Best you don't be telling what you seen up here."

We was looking at him, expecting him to go on and tell why we shouldn't say nothing, but all he said was, "See you, girl. See you, boy." And he walked on down the hill, coughing so loud we could hear him most of the way down.

Me and Bobby took a shortcut through the woods to get back home. The cold was starting to bite through our coats. My ears and fingers was already so numb, I couldn't tell if they was cold or not. When we come to the Indian's grave, Bobby hesitated for a minute. Then he straightened hisself up and walked on by like they weren't nothing to it, but I knowed it took a lot of guts for him to do that, scared as them boys is of that place.

While we was in the kitchen drinking hot chocolate and trying to get warm, we told Danny and Lou about what we seen. I noticed Mama listened with uncommon interest, but it weren't till later on that night I knowed why.

I was in the kitchen helping Mama fix supper when I seen Daddy and Mr. Weaver out in the front yard with their heads together like they was planning the next World War or something. I couldn't for the life of me figure what was going on. All during supper, Mama and Daddy kept looking at each other like they wanted to say something but couldn't let it out in front of everybody.

We was all sitting in the front room watching Jack Benny on television that night when there was a knock on the front door. It was Uncle Frank and Uncle Ariel. Daddy took them back to the kitchen, and I could hear them talking real soft. Then Daddy come back in the front room and asked me to come in the kitchen for a minute. Mama stopped Danny when he tried to follow.

"Annie, we need your help," Daddy said when we was in the kitchen. "We need to know exactly where it was you saw Old Man Fox this afternoon."

They all three was looking at me like I was something they found under a rock. "He was up the "H" Street hill, back behind Uncle Frank's when we first seen him," I said.

"Knowing that old man, he's got that thing sitting right on my property," Uncle Frank said, and he didn't look at all happy about it. His face was as red as Freddy Wayne's gets when he's mad about something.

Daddy patted me on the shoulder and said I been a big help, and I could tell Mama it was okay to explain. Then they all left, walking toward Uncle Frank's house.

Mama told me that Old Man Fox was moonshining. Daddy and Uncle Ariel and Uncle Frank was trying to help him by finding the still before the sheriff did. She said that some people wasn't very smart and had to be took care of like a baby. It weren't easy for me to understand how a grown up person could be that dumb. I reckon Old Man Fox was lucky to have Daddy and all them other men to care for him.

Mama seen the concerned look on my face, and said, "Don't worry about that old man, Annie. This has been going on for as long as I can remember." She patted me on the knee and smiled like we was conspiring on something. "We'll put a extra measure of brandy in his fruitcake." Then we both laughed, and that was that. Daddy come home about a hour later and winked real big at me and Mama. Old Man Fox was safe again.

Sunday night we had our Christmas Program at church. I got to be the head angel that year. That was a real honor, but I don't reckon there was anyone looked or sounded more like a angel than Lou did when she sang her song about the little baby Jesus. Danny did his usual. He was the only shepherd that tripped over his robe, but I reckon Jesus just loved him more for it. Danny ain't never been too sure on his feet.

After the program was over, Preacher Driggers give all the kids a orange and a apple. And the church give him and his wife a big turkey. People was happy all over the place. Laughing. Hugging. Wishing everbody a Merry Christmas and then hurrying on home to get busy with their own Christmas doings.

Ever since December come, our house had smelled like a bakery. Mama always made candy, cookies, fruitcakes, nut breads, and stuff like that for all the neighbors' Christmas presents. With Christmas getting closer, she was getting busier. Me and Lou wrapped all the packages, some of them still warm from the oven. I made a couple of things myself. For Bobby, I made a great big gingerbread man and decorated it with raisins and gumdrops and frosting. I ain't never been so proud of nothing. It was too pretty to eat, but I reckon that's just what Bobby would do to it.

I finally finished the scarf I was making for Be More. At first I thought I'd still be working on it for the next ten years, but I kept after it, and before I knowed it, all that yarn was a right nice neck scarf.

On Christmas Eve morning, the kitchen had a warm fruity smell as Mama took the cheesecloth wrappers off the fruitcakes and put them in boxes. Me and Lou wrapped them up, and put them on the table with all the other presents for me and Danny to deliver that afternoon. That was my favorite part of Christmas. I liked to give people things, but it always embarrassed me when they give things to me.

Soon as lunch was over, me and Danny headed on out to deliver our packages. First off, we went to Aunt Dorothy's house. Junior and Charles Edward was wrestling on the floor, right in front of the Christmas tree. Their house smelled almost as good as ours did. Aunt Dorothy thanked us for the present and said she'd send Junior and Charles Edward over later with ours. Aunt Dorothy was always running late. From the smell of their house, I could bet we'd be getting one of her delicious chocolate cakes.

Next, we went down to Aunt Virginia's. We give her a big box of cookies and fudge, and left Mr. Weaver's fruitcake with her 'cause we knowed he'd be there for Christmas. Then she give us a big box, probably the same thing we give her. When we was leaving, Freddy Wayne called out for us to wait a minute. He went in his room and come out with a little box that was wrapped real pretty.

"This is for you, Annie," he said, his face redder than I ever seen it.

I thanked him, and we all wished each other a Merry Christmas. I knowed what was in the package. It was the new hat he promised. From the curious looks Freddy Wayne was getting from Aunt Virginia, I had a feeling she would know all about it before the day was up. Poor Freddy Wayne.

We went down to Old Man Fox's place after that. They weren't no doubt about which package was his. It was the one what smelled so peculiar.

Since we was so close to home, we decided to stop by and leave off the boxes we got from Aunt Virginia and warm up for a minute. On the way up to our house, we passed by the Indian's grave, and like always, we stopped to look at it. I had been nagging at Danny ever since Halloween to tell me how come he weren't scared of that place like everybody else was.

"Come on, Danny," I said. "That can be my Christmas present. Just tell me. I swear I won't never tell no one."

"You'd tell," he said. "You're a girl, and girls always tell."

No! I swear ! I won't never, never, never tell." I was getting desperate.

"Swear to God?" he asked.

That was serious. We weren't allowed to swear to God, but I wanted to know so bad, I reckon I would of said most anything. "Swear to God!" I said, beaten.

He looked all around like he thought everybody he knowed was hiding in the bushes just waiting to hear why it was he weren't afraid of that place. Then he whispered in my ear. I looked at him and then at the Indian's grave, not knowing exactly how to react to a thing like that. Then I looked back at him and seen the laughter starting to bubble out of him. We both laughed till it felt like our ribs was gonna crack.

I reckon this is the place where I should be telling what it was Danny said in my ear, but I ain't gonna do it. I ain't never told no one. I swore to God!

Our next stop, after warming up at home, was Bobby's house. Mama give them a fruitcake and a big box of cookies and candy. I reckon she was trying to make up for there being no woman in the house. In spite of that, though, their house was decorated real nice, and I could smell a ham in the oven. Bobby was gonna have a Merry Christmas. I give him his gingerbread man, and he give me a present, too. It was the necklace made out of the pointy part of pinecones that his class at school made for their mothers. I could of cried, but I didn't. It was too happy a day for crying.

Next off we went down to Granny's. Billy and Jerry was in the kitchen, up to their elbows in cookie dough. Gene Autry was singing "Rudolf the Red-Nosed Reindeer" on the radio, and the whole house looked like Santa's workshop. There was wrapping paper, and ribbons, and wrapped up packages all over the place. We added one more and took one away with us when we left. Granny, waving to us from her kitchen door, looked just like a picture of Mrs. Santa Claus.

I weren't too happy to find Doc Elder's place closed up tight. I never knowed Doc Elder to close till late on Christmas Eve. I was worried that something might be wrong. I'd be sure to have Mama call and check on him as soon as we got home.

There was only one more stop, and no amount of worrying about Doc Elder or anyone else could dim that. Be More Happy! Mama told me before we left the house that I was to ask Be More to have Christmas Dinner with us. That made Christmas perfect. Everybody would be happy, no one alone.

Danny started dragging his feet soon as we walked into Be More's yard. "You ain't really gonna ask that old man to eat Christmas dinner with us, are you Annie?"

If looks could kill, Danny would of been six feet under right about then. "Mama said to," I snapped back at him. "Don't you never think about other people? How would you like to be all alone on Christmas Day?"

"Don't sound too bad to me," he answered back, but what did a seven year old boy know about anything?

Be More opened up the back door soon as I knocked, like he'd been standing there waiting for someone to knock on his door.

"Annie! Danny! Come on in. I was hoping you would come by." I was glad to see him in such a good mood.

His kitchen was all light and cheery. It smelled just as good as any I been in all that day, and the reason for it was right there in front of the stove, wearing a big white apron.

"Doc Elder!" me and Danny said at the same time.

I went on talking while Danny stood there with his mouth hanging open. "We was just down to your place. I was wondering where you was," I said.

Be More sat me and Danny down at the table there in the kitchen and give us each a big mug of hot cider. While we was sipping at it, Doc Elder told us about their plans for Christmas Day. Be More didn't say nothing, but the twinkle in his eyes told me everything I needed to know. Doc said they were going to eat Christmas Dinner there at Be More's house and then go down to Children's Hospital and give out candy.

I don't know how or when Doc Elder and Be More got to be such good friends, but knowing Doc Elder, Be More didn't have no choice in the matter. Doc Elder could make friends with a grizzly bear.

Be More took us into his front room and showed us his tree. It was ever' bit as pretty as the one in our front room at home. He pulled a package out from under it, give it to me, and asked me to open it. I tore the paper away to reveal a beautiful brass picture frame. Behind the glass was an embroidered picture of children playing in the woods, and beneath the children was a little poem that read:

> *Happy hearts and happy faces,*
> *Happy play in grassy places,*
> *That was how, in ancient ages,*
> *Children grew to kings and sages.*
> —R.L. Stevenson

He told me that his mother had made it for him, and how it hung in his room for so many years, and now he wanted me to have it.

I couldn't say nothing 'cause I was just about to cry, so I gave Be More a big hug. Then I gave him and Doc Elder their presents. There was a lot of fuss about how nice everything was. I can't recall ever being happier. Before we left his house, Be More stuffed all of Danny's pockets with candy and give us a basket of fruit to take home to the family.

All our Merry Christmas work was done and we was on our way back home. The woods was so cold you could hear things popping and snapping when the wind blew, *and it did blow!* I seen a bright red cardinal eating off one of the pinecone bird feeders we hung up. The sun was sinking behind the hill, and it was getting colder. But I had a warm feeling inside and was thinking on how good it felt to give people things. Then Danny started to laugh that devilish laugh of his. He said, "You forgot! I didn't! I could of reminded you, but I didn't."

Danny never was one to pay attention to what was going on around him! He thought I forgot to invite Be More to our house. I didn't say nothing. I figured if that's what it took to make Danny happy, he was welcome to it. Besides, I didn't want to argue. My teeth was getting cold and it was Christmas!

Chapter 20

A blink of the eye and fifty-three years later ...

The funeral train rolled on through the woods and along the river. It had been such a cold dreary winter, and now a funeral to top it off. How perfect!

A knock on my compartment door followed by Lou's voice brought me back to the present. "Annie, are you awake?"

"Of course I'm awake. Do you think I sleep all day?" I said as I opened the door to let her in. Lou looked fantastic. Almost sixty-five and could still turn heads anywhere she went, even if they didn't know who she was. "You didn't eat lunch yet, did you?" she asked as she sat down across from me next to the window. "I'm so hungry I could eat the bark off one of those trees out there!"

"I'm ready if you are," I said. "Do you want to go to the dining car? Maybe some of the guys will be there."

"Didn't you get a note under your door?" As she asked, she got up to see and picked up the envelope on the floor. "You have to pay attention, Annie. What were you doing? Dreaming up the plot for your next book?"

"No," I said, looking out the window. "I was just reminiscing. Didn't you see those kids on the riverbank back there? They reminded me of when we were kids."

Lou smiled as she opened the envelope and read, "'Luncheon will be served in the Club Car at 12:30 pm. If this is not convenient, please make arrangements with your porter.' Since you obviously didn't 'make arrangements with your porter,' I suggest we head for the club car."

I opened the closet to get my purse and a jacket and was promptly reminded, "You won't need all that. We are the only ones on this train and Jerry made a special point of saying that we were his guests. That means no tipping, no paying for anything. This is his show, Hon, let him do what he wants."

"Okay," I said. "I've just been so distracted. Billy is the first one of us to die." I put my jacket back on the hook and opened my purse, saying facetiously, "Do you suppose it will be okay if I take my glasses?"

"Who takes care of you when I'm not around?" Lou asked as she laughed and closed the door behind us.

As we entered the club car, we were greeted by soft music and the warm, gentle voices and laughter of good friends and family. It appeared we were the last to arrive. What luxury! Jerry had really outdone himself. But then, Billy was the only family he had. Of course, we are all like family, but it's never quite the same. We all worried and fussed over Jerry as if we had been blood kin, and had done so ever since Billy came back from Viet Nam.

Billy had just finished med school when he was drafted and sent to Viet Nam. That would have been fine, but as often happens in war, Billy was never the same when he got home. Some horrific rescue attempt that had gone wrong had left only the shell of our Billy to roam the forests of northern California. Jerry liked to have never found him, and when he did, his life was forever changed just as much as Billy's had been. It was Jerry who went to practically every florist in northern California and agreed to reimburse them for anything they bought from the homeless. Billy gathered ferns and sold them to local florists. It was Jerry who took off from work the third week of every month and dressed in his homeless duds, went into the forest to find his brother, and make his life as easy as possible. It was Jerry who found Billy wrapped in a cardboard box, dead from exposure. And now, it is Jerry who is taking him home to Arkansas to be buried with Granny and Gramps.

Lou and I served ourselves from the buffet that had been set up and joined the group at the big table. It was wonderful to see everybody. That was the first time we had all been together at the same time since Be More Happy's funeral just before I left for college in 1961.

The train arrived in Little Rock just before noon the next day. The drive to the cemetery was somber. And then the funeral. It was a moving ceremony with only those of us from the train and an Army chaplin to do the eulogy. And far off on the hillside, a twenty-one-gun salute was sounded at some prearranged time. Billy had been a war hero. Even though the mission that brought him down had failed, he had saved many, many lives prior to that. He will always be our hero.

Before the day was over, we cried many tears, both happy and sad. Then we said goodbye and vowed to meet again *before* the next funeral. It was doubly sad because we all knew our promises would get caught in the tangle of everyday life and we would end up at another funeral somewhere down the line.

Be More had been on all our minds that sad day. Even though he had been dead for more than forty years, he was just as certainly in attendance at Billy's funeral as any one of us. He was part of each of us.

Shortly after that Christmas when he and Doc Young became such good friends, Be More had set up trust funds for each of the kids in our little community. Nobody knew about this until Freddy Wayne and Junior graduated high school and received letters from Be More's attorney. From then on, we each received a letter telling us about our individual trust funds upon graduation.

However, the real gift from Be More came to us daily, throughout the years. He taught each of us that nothing was impossible. He taught us to dream, and then he taught us how to make dreams come true, simply by believing in them. He taught us that believing in dreams took real courage. We were probably the only kids in Arkansas who were quoting Goethe in junior high school. Goethe was Be More's favorite philosopher. When Be More had shared, "Are you in earnest, seize this very moment. Boldness has genius, power and magic in it," we learned we could do anything.

Be More taught each of us that all we had to do to get what we wanted out of life was to go for it. "Believe it and it is yours," he told us. And we believed. Jerry had been in love with trains all his life. He is now CEO of the biggest railroad in America. *Jerry believed.* Freddy Wayne didn't want to go to college. He wanted to play ball, and man, did he play ball! When he retired from the Cardinals, he used Be More Happy's trust fund to start his own business building log houses in Colorado. *Freddy Wayne believed.* Junior wouldn't go to college either. All he was interested in was music. He now lives in Nashville, Tennessee and not only plays the guitar, but makes them. His guitars are sought after from people all over the world. *Junior believed.* Jimmy went to school at Berkley. His passion was flying. When he graduated with his business degree, he went back home to Arkansas and started an air charter service. *Jimmy believed.* Bobby, who grew up cleaning out chicken coops, now owns chicken houses all over Arkansas, and sells chickens all over America. *Bobby believed.* Charles Edward was in love with music just as his brother was, only his affair with music was in the form of dance. Modern dance. He has studios all over the East Coast and the West Coast. He is the modern dance guru in America. *Charles Edward believed.* Lou, again, no college but lots of voice, charm, and style lessons. She is one of the nation's top country western singer/songwriters. *Lou believed.* That brings it to me. College? Yes. I write for a living. I live it, and breathe it. Also teach it. It is my very soul. *I believed*. Last, but not least, Danny. I think I envy him more than any of the others. When he retired from the Navy, he moved to Apalachicola, Florida and builds boats. People come from all over the world to buy his boats. *Danny believed*.

Each of us had our own passion. Be More taught us that nothing is stronger than a dream. The trust funds were merely the wind that sent us soaring into the clouds. Be More's little poem was right. The ten children who grew up in those woods with their *happy play in grassy places* have all become kings and sages in one way or the other. We believed in ourselves. We worked hard and made our dreams come true. He never said it would be easy!

Made in the USA
Lexington, KY
10 March 2010